Who Killed
Olive Souffle?

Who Killed
Olive Souffle?

Margaret Benoit

**LEARNING
TRIANGLE
PRESS**

*Connecting
kids, parents, and teachers
through learning*

An imprint of McGraw-Hill

New York San Francisco Washington, D.C. Auckland Bogotá Caracas
Lisbon London Madrid Mexico City Milan Montreal New Delhi
San Juan Singapore Sydney Tokyo Toronto

McGraw-Hill

A Division of The McGraw·Hill Companies

This novel is a work of fiction. Names, characters, places, and incidents are either the product of the author's imagination or are used fictitiously. Any resemblence to actual events or locales or persons, living or dead, is entirely coincidental.

Library of Congress Cataloging-in-Publication Data applied for.

1 2 3 4 5 6 7 8 9 0 DOC/DOC 9 0 2 1 0 9 8 7 (hc)

1 2 3 4 5 6 7 8 9 0 DOC/DOC 9 0 2 1 0 9 8 7 (pbk)

ISBN 0-07-006310-9 (hc)

ISBN 0-07-006275-7 (pbk)

The sponsoring editor for this book was Judith Terrill-Breuer, the manuscript editor was Judy Gitenstein, the editing supervisor was Patricia V. Amoroso, and the production supervisor was Claire B. Stanley. It was set in Times Ten Roman by Jaclyn J. Boone of McGraw-Hill's Professional Book Group in Hightstown, New Jersey.

Printed and bound by R. R. Donnelley & Sons Company.

In memory of Louise
and the force behind the cookbooks

Special thanks to Daniel Matticks,
San Diego County Medical Examiner's office

Table of Contents

1

The Vacation and the Deer

I WAS HUNGRY! I had a craving for chocolate chip cookies that just wouldn't quit. I'm not talking about one or two cookies. I was thinking more along the lines of one or two *dozen*.

"Are we there yet?" I asked. "No," I answered. Silly question—I was the one driving. We had at least another hour before we got to my cabin in the mountains. My name is Angel Cardoni. I'm a homicide detective with City P.D.—and one of the few women in our department. I'm five-foot-six with brown hair and brown eyes. I'm very good at my job, but last night had just about done me in. I still couldn't get the images out of my head as I thought back to . . .

Wednesday, 3 A.M. "I tell you, Cardoni," Greyson was saying as we examined the body, "you're in over your head here. He was shot at point-blank range. Someone was settling an overdue account."

"Thanks a bunch, Greyson," I told him. "If I need a lecture, I'll remember to call you at three in the morning and ask for your expert opinion." The nerve of the guy! I had more experience as a detective than he did and *he* was lecturing *me*? We were in the middle of the victim's living room. The guy's roommate had arrived home to find the victim facedown on the sofa.

We had gotten the call at 2:37 A.M. Dispatch put it through and we spent the next hour asking questions. We stood around the hallway, not wanting to disturb possible evidence as we waited for Marisa Flores, the photographer. The fingerprints guy couldn't really do anything until then. The medical examiner's van was parked outside in the driveway, also waiting.

Marisa Flores finally arrived in a flurry of equipment cases and really good excuses. The sudden bright glare of her flashbulb became a red spot in my eyes wherever I looked. I felt lightheaded and certain that if I didn't get some food and sleep soon . . . I didn't know what I would do. I only knew that I had had enough.

It was after eight on Wednesday morning when I finally rolled into my driveway. Home is a modest two-story cottage a few blocks from the beach. Miro barked like crazy from the upper deck.

"What a nutty dog!" I exclaimed as I walked up the path to the door and put my key into the lock. When I opened the door, Miro exploded from the entryway, almost knocking me over.

"Is that tail gonna fall off or what?" I asked as she thumped it on the floor. Miro was my welcome home committee. She was always happy to see me.

"Hup! Hup!" I patted my chest.

Up she jumped, paws on my stomach, and aimed a slobbery dog kiss on my cheek.

"Good girl! Good girl, Miro!"

It was great to be home. I dropped the keys on the hall table.

"What'cha been doin', girl? Sleeping? You lucky dog, you!"

I took off my windbreaker and kicked off my shoes on my way to the stairs. Miro scampered up, almost knocking me over with her enthusiasm.

"All right, all right, we'll take a nap," I said as she barked happily.

"*Nien!* No!" She understands some German commands. Of course—she's a German Shepherd.

Upstairs, she settled on the bed quietly. It hadn't been slept in for two days. I had crashed on the sofa the day before, too tired to make it upstairs. Now I collapsed into bed and slept soundly for the first time in weeks.

The world managed to function without me for ten hours or so. It would have to function without me for another ten days, too. I was officially on vacation.

Dinner was a bowl of cereal in front of the evening news. I crunched on the flakes, missing every other word the newscaster was saying as I listened to the report of the homicide I had just investigated.

Suddenly, the walls seemed to close in on me. I looked around the room. Then I looked at myself in the mirror on the wall. I was wearing a navy-blue City Police Department T-shirt and faded jeans that fit comfortably. I usually like what I see in the mirror. That night, a tired face looked back at me. My shoulder-length hair needed brushing. My eyes looked tired. I needed a real vacation.

"Miro, we're going for a ride."

She barked ecstatically.

We were packed and good to go in an hour. I took some warm clothes, some cookbooks, some CDs, and my oil paints. I lugged everything out to the car, Miro yapping merrily at my heels. My mail would fall through the door slot and a timer was set to turn on and off the lights, stereo, and TV.

My head cleared and the knot in my left shoulder began to ease up as we got farther from the smog, the noise, and the crime scenes. The sky was a black-gray that reminded me of a wind-tossed sea. Snow was on the way—I could feel it. Miro was out cold on the backseat, wiggling her paws, dreaming doggy dreams. I drove, she slept . . .

"Hello folks, this is Late Night Les. You just heard Lila Houston's cover of a Kim Turbine song. And now for the weather. It looks like more of that flaky white stuff in the mountains through tomorrow."

Big news, I thought—it had been snowing for the past hour. The wipers made a hypnotic rhythm as they cleared an arc on my windshield. "Might be a bummer for you Les, but my plans include that snow," I said to the radio. I couldn't wait to hit those slopes.

The road dipped and rose across a landscape of lonely ridges. They made me think of a pie crust. I was getting hungry. Why not? It was 11:00 P.M.

Miro stretched, pushing her long legs into the back of my seat.

"You hungry, too?" I asked.

She grunted once and fell asleep, lost again in her doggy dreams.

The car headlights sliced through the darkness, and thick snowflakes glittered in the beams. I hadn't seen another vehicle for over an hour. *I wouldn't want to break down out here*, I thought with a shudder.

Suddenly a deer appeared in front of the car. I swerved to avoid hitting it and drove the car straight into the embankment on the other side of the road. Miro howled in confusion as she was flung to one side of the car.

2

"I Ham Olive Souffle"

NOTHING BROKEN, no blood. I was dizzy, but otherwise we were both fine. Then the adrenaline rush came. My arms and legs felt warm and jumpy and my heart pounded as if I had just run the City Marathon. Miro panted heavily in the backseat, pausing now and then to regroup. She looked at me as if she were thinking, *Just what do you call that maneuver?*

The deer was long gone. It had seemed less surprised than I was, almost as if it made a habit of stepping in front of tourists' cars in the middle of the night.

"Getting out is going to be an experience," I said to Miro. Putting the car in reverse did nothing. The snow was as high as the windshield.

"Oh, great. Ho, ho, ho. 'Tis the season to be stuck in the snow." It was so cold, my sarcasm froze in midair. The wipers were still going as I peered out. I could see a light in the distance. It looked like someone was home.

I cracked my door open, put my feet on the ground, and stood up shakily. Miro jumped out and stretched her legs, as if this were a regular walk in the park. She was ready for anything.

I slung my pack over my shoulder, then grabbed the other bag and a flashlight. I left a note under the wiper in case a passing motorist or state trooper found the car.

As we trudged along, I could feel the snow getting into my boots. I noticed how dark it was without city lights or freeway traffic. I mean, it was *dark*. And the only sound was the sudden snap of a tree branch, breaking from its load of snow.

The house seemed to get bigger as we approached it. It was two stories high, and made of logs.

The snowfall dulled my senses and hushed the sounds of our movements as we made our way to the door. We crossed over fresh footprints.

"Good, someone must be here," I said to Miro, more to hear my own voice than anything. I stood at what looked like a service entrance. I knocked loudly. I checked my watch: 11:38 P.M. Not too late, I hoped.

I glanced at the doorbell, wondering if I should ring it, when I heard footsteps. The door opened suddenly.

"*Oui?* Yes?" A petite woman in white pants and a black sweater stood at the door. She had wild orange hair and vivid green eyes.

"Zees ees not a deli-verry?" She spoke with a thick French accent.

"No, sorry to disappoint you." I was ready to launch into a plea to call a tow truck when the woman saw Miro.

"*Oh, quel ange!*" she said as she bent to pet her. "She is an angel!"

As if on cue, Miro did her standard "aren't I cute" routine. The woman seemed to go for it. She murmured sweet nothings into Miro's ear.

I felt kind of bad interrupting her, but I had no choice. "I'm stuck in the snow and was wondering if I could call a tow truck or get some help pushing the car."

She considered the situation for a moment, then stepped back from the door and said, "*Non, non, non.* Ees too cold for you. You will stay 'ere tonight. Take care of your car in the morning."

I breathed a sigh of relief. "Thank you so much," I said as we stepped into the kitchen. The wonderful smells of cooking put Miro and me both into sensory overdrive.

"I'm Angel Cardoni. This is Miro."

"I ham Olive Souffle," the lady with the wild orange hair said as we shook hands. She stooped to shake a paw with Miro.

A single light was on at a desk overloaded with papers. Gleaming countertops and stainless steel ovens sat in the shadows along one wall. The floors were spotless.

She turned suddenly. "Would you like a cup of *cafe*?"

"No, thank you, though," I said.

"*Alors*. Perhaps some *soup aux pois*, pea soup, then?" she asked.

My stomach growled. "If it's not too much trouble, I would love some," I answered.

"And Miro, she would like a midnight snack, *non*?" Olive Souffle asked.

"*Oui*," I answered, "thank you very much."

Miro knew we were talking about her. She heard the word "snack" and twisted her head to one side.

Olive Souffle walked over to a huge refrigerator and pulled out a heavy iron pot. As Miro and I both drooled, Olive warmed up the soup and sliced some bread.

I wandered around the kitchen. The fire crackled and sparked in the fireplace. Trophies stood shining on the mantle. They were cooking awards, mostly with Olive Souffle's name. "She must be an outstanding cook, Miro," I whispered.

I looked at her desk. She had been preparing a grocery list, probably for the next "deli-verry." Boy, I must have been tired. I was starting to think in a French accent.

I was right—the grocery list had the next week's date on it. My stomach roared again unexpectedly as I read the list: a variety of fruits, vegetables and legumes, an endless assortment of baking ingredients, chicken, and fish.

Suddenly a steaming bowl of pea soup was in front of me with two thick pieces of French bread. Miro was treated to cold cuts.

"Thank you so much," I said.

Olive Souffle sat down across from me and took up her pen. She glanced at me as I took my first noisy slurp. I felt embarrassed but the soup was the best I had ever tasted. She smiled and turned to her list.

"You're a cook, then?" I said to break the silence.

"No, I ham a chef," she said proudly. "There is a difference."

"Oh. This is great soup, by the way," I said. "I want to thank you for your generosity."

"It ees not a problem," she said.

"I hope you understand that I don't make a habit of banging on people's doors in the middle of the night. I was driving when a deer stepped into the middle of

11

the road," I said.

"How terrible!" she exclaimed, "You are not hurt?"

"No, but my car's stuck in a snowbank. I guess I could have been killed with the impact." I suddenly realized I was very lucky to be alive.

"You are very lucky to be alive," Olive Souffle said, as if she could hear my thoughts. "You have stayed with us in the past?" she inquired.

"No, I've never stayed here before," I admitted. I had probably driven by the place more than a dozen times, though.

"Bear Lodge is something old, something new," she murmured. "It was built as a log cabin over one hundred years ago by a miner. A developer built the rest of it. It is now a country inn."

"With the best food in the mountains," I said enthusiastically. The soup had been so good that I felt like licking the bowl. But I managed to restrain myself.

Miro had to agree. She was basking in the glow of the fire.

"I can't thank you enough," I began again.

"Don't be silly," Olive said with a wave of her hand. "It is a *plaisir*, a pleasure, to cook for someone who can appreciate it." She smiled again. "One day maybe you can do a favor for me."

She reached over to pet Miro's shaggy fur. "This Miro," she said, "she is yours for how long now?"

"I got her in the pound about two years ago," I answered, warming to the subject. "She's three now, and full-grown."

Miro lifted her head and a sleepy eye looked in my direction.

"She's so smart. She knows we're talking about her," I said proudly.

"Ah, *oui*," Olive Souffle remarked. "She is a police dog?"

"No, actually. She's not a police dog—wait a minute! How did you know?" I asked.

"Your gun is more apparent than you think," Olive said pointing to the bulge under my sweater.

"Why did you let me in? I could have been a burglar!" I exclaimed.

"I ham a good judge of character. Don't you agree, Miro?"

Miro only stretched.

Olive looked at the clock over the mantle. "It's late. You must be tired. In the morning everything will seem clear. Fix your car and go your way. In the meantime, you must get some sleep," she said softly.

She pointed to the door at the other end of the kitchen. I followed Olive Souffle, Miro close at my heels. We opened a set of huge doors and we were suddenly in a lobby area.

"Please sign," Olive said, indicating the register. "You are in number 12, west wing, on the right at the top of the stairs." She handed me a key.

"Thank you so much," I said. "What do I owe you?"

"Fifty dollars," she said. "It ees out of season. We are not open for two more days."

As I trudged up the carpeted stairs, I heard her whisper "*bonne nuit*," good night, as she turned to go back to the kitchen.

I looked down the dark corridor. The Emergency Exit light was on at the far end of the hall. A ribbon of light shone under one of the doors. It went out almost as soon as I noticed it. *Another night owl*, I thought as I unlocked my door.

Miro pushed her way through my legs and jumped neatly onto the pillow.

"I don't think so," I said as I pushed her off.

She groaned softly as she nestled onto the blankets stacked at the foot of the bed.

A small room, it had fresh sheets and blankets. It was bitterly cold, compared to the cozy warmth of the kitchen. The sudden change chilled me to a teeth-chattering clatter.

I dove under the covers at 12:47 A.M. and melted into sleep when my head touched the pillow. I slept soundly until the screams began.

3

Deep Freeze

THE SCREAMS rang in my head. I jumped into my clothes, instinctively grabbed my gun, and ran down the stairs with Miro close at my heels. We huffed it to the kitchen, where it seemed that the screams had started. My heart pounded. Was I having a nightmare? It had to be. But this one seemed so real.

Adrenaline pumped as I walked around the kitchen, absorbing everything. Miro panted as she trotted around, searching the shadows with me. I tried a light switch. Nothing. The power was out. There were a few emergency lights on. The warm glow I remembered from only a few hours earlier was gone.

I looked at my watch. It was 6:00 A.M.

One pale beam of light shone on the floor from a hidden room. No, it was a walk-in freezer. I heard ragged breathing, gasps of horror, and sobs from the doorway.

Miro sniffed hesitantly, her claws clicking on the bare floor. My shoes made a crunching, grating sound as I slipped on a brownish gritty substance. I entered the walk-in freezer. A young woman and a man were leaning over a body dressed in black and white. I recognized the wild orange hair. Olive Souffle.

The man and the woman stood up suddenly and looked at me in amazement. "Who are you?" the woman said.

"Angel Cardoni, City P.D.," I replied tersely.

"Who called you?" the man asked.

"No one. I'm a guest here," I answered.

A look that I couldn't quite figure out passed between the man and woman. If we weren't standing near a body at 6:00 in the morning in a walk-in freezer, I'd think there was something romantic going on between the two.

"You're definitely not what I would expect," the man said finally. *Oh, I get it.* I thought. Even with a badge and ID, people don't always believe that I'm a homicide detective. I'm not what people expect. They look for the overweight, older guy who's been on the force for a century, who's only one fast-food meal away from a heart attack.

"Sorry. Next time I'll send someone from Central Casting," I said as I bent down to examine the body.

"She's dead," the woman said in a flat voice, twisting one strand of blond hair around a finger.

I placed my finger on Olive's neck to check for a pulse. There was none. Her eyes were shut and her skin was cold. Yes, she was definitely dead.

I stood up. "My name's Norm Adams," the man said even before I had a chance to ask. "Patty was opening up the freezer door when she screamed. I dropped a case of cabbages!" he exclaimed.

I looked around the freezer, and saw that about a dozen red cabbages had rolled in all directions. *Later for your cabbages*, I thought. I got down on my knees to examine Olive Souffle. Her brilliant orange hair was in disarray, most of it covering her face. Her lips were pale—as if her body had been quickly drained of life and color. Her delicate hands were rigid.

She was lying on her left side as if she had been flung there. It didn't look like there had been a struggle, though—her shirt was still tucked in, and her sweater was neatly in place. I noticed a circular bruise on her right wrist.

I also noticed something strange—a small amount of clear frozen liquid on the floor near her chest. I looked on the sweater and the shirt. There was a tiny patch of blood around an opening in her shirt, about three centimeters in diameter. The blood had frozen on her skin in the cold air of the freezer.

I looked around the freezer. I saw Norm's dolly loaded with cases of produce and the cabbages on the freezer floor. I looked at him and judged him to be average height, average weight—and average intelligence, considering his concern for his cabbages. Norm was dressed for the outdoors. He had on a large wool knit hat that partly covered his long black hair, a thick jacket, and boots.

I glanced at the woman named Patty. She looked at me through a veil of tears. She twirled the same strand of hair around and around. I wondered if she was dizzy from all that twirling.

"I'm Patricia Bordeaux," the woman said between sobs. She was dressed in jeans, clunky combat boots, and a white shirt that cooks wear. Her left ear was decked out with five or six earrings. "I'm really going to miss Olive."

"Nice to meet you," I said. "I mean, I'm sorry to meet you under these circumstances. And, I'm sorry to bother you now, but I wonder—do you have a camera?" I know it was kind of awkward, but I had to get down to business. Any crime scene needs to be photographed.

There was a loud knock at the door, then footsteps scuffed toward us. "Business sure is starting early here!"

We all turned to look at the newcomer. He was a heavyset man with a long beard that fell straight from his chin. In his thick hat with ear flaps, he made quite a sight as he stood in the doorway. Miro sniffed at him suspiciously.

"Wha . . .?" He stopped short as he saw Olive's body.

"Bert, I just found her lying here," Patty wailed. "She's dead."

"What happened? She can't be dead!" he protested. Then he noticed me. "Who's she?" he asked.

"Cardoni, City P.D.," I responded as I looked back at Olive's body.

"You guys are fast, huh?" He seemed to think for a moment. "Wait a minute, you're out of your jurisdiction. Aren't the sheriffs supposed to take care of things here?"

"I'm on vacation," I said. *Some vacation*, I thought with a sigh.

"Cardoni, this is Bert Paltry," Norm Adams said. "He runs the local store."

"What can I do to help?" Bert asked.

"Everybody could help by stepping outside of the freezer and not using it until the medical examiner gets here," I said.

"That might be a problem," Patty said. "The phone lines are out. We can't call anyone."

"Hey, it's the nineties," Bert said as he whipped out a cell phone and offered it to me.

I accepted the phone.

"I really have to ask you to leave the freezer," I said again.

"What if we need to come in here to get our ingredients?" Patty asked.

Before I could answer, another voice rang out. "What's going on in here?" A burly guy entered the freezer. He had dark brown hair and brown eyes. The name tag on his white cook's shirt read *Caesar*. He looked over the scene and then stared at me with a piercing gaze. His deep brown eyes held questions.

"Where is everybody?" a voice boomed from the kitchen.

Wow! It was getting to be a regular Grand Central station here. Fortunately, the last voice really commanded attention. As if on cue, Patricia, Norm, Bert, and Caesar all left the freezer. I was alone with another dead body. On my vacation.

I looked at Miro sitting in the doorway. She looked back, as if thinking, *Okay, now what?* Slowly, I punched in the numbers on the cell phone and called the local sheriff's office. The roads were being cleared as we spoke, the dispatcher told me. It would take a good half-day to get out to the inn.

"Dead bodies never look like they do in the movies, do they, girl?" I whispered to Miro. She whined. She can read me like a book and she could tell I was shook up. No matter how many crime scenes I've worked on, corpses up-close give me the creeps.

"Do you see this, Miro?" I whispered. "Olive Souffle's hair is orange but the one hair that I see on her shirt is black."

I noticed that some of the gritty substance I had slipped on in the kitchen was also near Olive's shoes, and that the heels on her shoes were scuffed badly. Maybe she had been dragged into the freezer.

"No, I can't write the story until I see all the details," I said out loud. Miro looked at me, her head tilted to one side.

I forced myself to look around again.

Yes, there was definitely something strange near her head. I could see a few crystals of a white substance in and around her hair. I also noticed a bump on her left temple.

I checked her pockets. I found a wadded tissue, an aspirin, and the crumpled grocery list that I had seen on her desk the night before. I looked at the list and noticed something I hadn't seen the night before. The word *pois*—pea in French—had been circled.

Had I just not noticed it, or had the word been circled after I had my bowl of pea soup?

In the same right pocket was a pen. From her pants pocket I found a creased note that read: *Your expiration date is soon. Soufle.*

A death threat! "The plot thickens, Miro," I said softly as my number one fan watched. "Or, perhaps in this case, I should say 'the soup thickens.'"

A small commotion broke my concentration and there was Bert, standing in the freezer doorway. Miro groaned and it threatened to turn into a growl. Bert froze and pointed to Miro with a frightened look in his eyes.

"Did you find a camera?" I asked.

"Someone will bring you a camera in a few minutes," he replied. "I thought you might like to know, huh, that I've got information that can definitely be of some use to you."

"And what would that be?" I asked, shifting impatiently. Miro growled again, as if she liked the effect she was having on Bert. *Yeah, and what would that be?* she seemed to be thinking.

"I think it's real suspicious, huh, that Olive dies just before she gets another award and just before the owner of the lodge was getting ready to sell her the place for a song," he said.

"Thank you, Bert, for leaping right over to

the motive. Right now, though, I'd better begin my investigation with scientific facts. And here's the first fact, Bert," I said. "Olive Souffle didn't just die. She was murdered."

4

Too Many Cooks

BERT'S JAW DROPPED like trash from a leaky paper bag.

"Are you sure?" he sputtered. He looked at my face. I was using my stone-cold, don't-mess-with-me look.

"Miro looks kind of antsy right now. Did I mention that she loves to chase people?" Bert looked at Miro. His whole expression read *huh?*

"I'd think it best that you wait outside for me so I can finish up in here." Miro took this moment to yawn a big wolf yawn and lick her chops.

Bert spun around and zipped out of the freezer.

"I have a camera here!" said a loud voice from the kitchen, and a new arrival entered the freezer. "We keep one in the kitchen to photograph our chef's masterpieces."

Before I could stop him, he had walked all over the freezer, snapping photos of the body as if he had been doing it all his life. His long, slender fingers focused the camera confidently. I could see his mouth working behind the camera. He licked his chapped lips in the cold. His short black hair was slicked back from his face. If anyone were to throw up on his shirt, I'd never notice. The pattern screamed for help.

I blocked his path. "You are?" I asked, preventing him from walking near the victim's head.

"Miserable, now that Olive's gone," he said mournfully.

Oh, pul-ease.

"Walter Peace. I manage this lodge. I don't believe we've met before?" His eyes shone brightly, as if a death in a freezer in his lodge were routine.

"You're so right, we haven't met," I said sweetly. "Detective Cardoni, P.D. Could you please wait outside with the others?"

"So what do you think happened to her?" he asked as if he hadn't heard me.

"Did you know the phone lines are down and the power's out?" he went on, trying to sound helpful. For some reason, I doubted his motives.

"Yup, and there's a generator keeping the food lockers cool," I said slowly.

"Correct," he said. "And you are the only registered guest—out of season, I might add.

We aren't open for another two days." His eyes rested on Miro, who had moved to an out-of-the-way spot by the door. She stared back at him, as if daring him to challenge her.

"What is that *thing* doing in my freezer?" he exclaimed indignantly as he pointed to her.

"That *thing* is my dog and she goes where I go," I said.

"I'm terribly allergic to dogs!" he almost shouted.

"You can wait outside with the others," I suggested helpfully.

He took me up on that one.

I had work to do. I would need to wait until the medical examiner got there to begin officially processing the evidence. In the meantime, I could take small samples of everything and perform some tests with rudimentary equipment.

"Miro, we're back to work here," I said.

She looked at me, her head to one side. We walked to the door. I stationed her outside it and shut Olive's body away for safekeeping. I turned around to face the kitchen and all eyes turned toward me. The conversation stopped.

In addition to Caesar Martinez, Patty Bordeaux, Walter Peace, Bert Paltry, and Norm Adams, there were two other people that I hadn't met. Sharry Genese was the groundskeeper and general maintenance person. She was stocky and muscular, but otherwise average-looking.

There was Sam Burnie, another cook, who held in his hand a pastry that looked like a carving. He was tall and lanky, a free spirit, or at least that's what his tie-dyed chef's shirt seemed to say.

"Well, what happened?" Caesar asked, his voice filled with worry.

"I won't go out on a limb and say what I think happened to Olive just yet. I'm advising all of you to stay together in groups, and not to wander off by yourselves."

They looked at each other. It was as if I could see the news sink in. I watched everyone get very scared. If there was an actor among them, it would be hard to find him or her.

"I'll need a few things to conduct my investigation," I said.

"What do you need?" Sam asked.

"Chopping board, sharp knife, clean glass containers, stainless steel pot, glass plate, matches, coffee filters, clean glass jars, paper bags, paper towels, coat hanger."

"Got all those except the coat hanger," Sam said.

"I can get that," Sharry volunteered as she left the kitchen.

"What exactly do you plan on doing?"

Walter asked.

"I'll run a few tests to figure out what happened here and who's responsible," I replied.

"Don't you need sophisticated equipment to do that?" he asked. "And, aren't you supposed to be questioning all of us as to our whereabouts?"

"Mr. Peace," I began, "The first rule of an investigation is that an investigator is only as good as his or her information. What good is it for me to ask each of you where you were between the hours of 12:40 and 6:00 A.M.? You can say what you want. If there are no alibis, it becomes my hunch against your word. That's not an investigation. That is a witch hunt."

Patty stepped back, her arms crossed defensively. Norm set his jaw in a hard line, as if he were angry. Caesar raised his brows in amazement.

Bert nodded, his chest puffed up with self-importance. He was now a part of something important, a murder investigation.

"The medical examiner will be here soon," I continued. "We should have this wrapped up in a few days—if," I added, "the person who committed the murder left us enough evidence. . ."

"Here's the coat. . ." Sharry announced as she returned to the kitchen from the direction of the lobby. She stopped in her tracks when she heard my last words.

"What about our guests?" Walter fretted.

"We do open in two days," Caesar said.

"I want to remind everyone that any negative publicity that this brings us. . .well, it can't do us any good," Walter droned.

"What about *Olive*?" Patty cut in with a small voice.

"What *about* Olive?" Sam echoed, looking at Walter.

"The body will remain in its position until the medical examiner arrives. No one should go into the freezer for anything," I said with authority.

"What about our food shipments?" Caesar asked. "We have guests to serve in two days. We have to get some things started."

The others nodded in agreement.

"Aren't there other freezers?" I asked.

"Two other freezers, three refrigerators," Patty said as she pointed behind me.

"I still haven't finished delivering everything," Norm said.

"I'm sure you can make everything fit in the other freezers," I said.

"Okay," he said, sounding uncertain.

He walked off with Patty, Sam, and Sharry.

"I want to make it clear to everyone that the freezer holding Olive's body is off-limits. All the food in there is now considered contaminated and cannot be used."

Everyone seemed to accept that bit of information reasonably well. I, on the other hand, wasn't comfortable with the situation. I was stranded and surrounded by one or more killers.

"As I said, everyone here should stick close together," I said. "This killer might strike again. Anyone could be a victim. Or, for that matter . . ." I looked around for dramatic effect before I continued.

"Any one of you could also *be* the killer."

5

The Investigation Begins

I LOOKED AT MY WATCH. It was 6:47 A.M.
I stationed Miro outside the freezer door.
"Don't let anyone get past you to tamper
with the evidence," I said softly so no one
could hear.

I made a quick trip upstairs to my room
and grabbed my evidence kit. No good
homicide detective should be without one,
even on vacation. I padded back down the
stairs, welcoming the pale sun's rays in
the dark corridor.

In the kitchen, everyone was busy doing
something or other. Someone had started
a fire in the fireplace and the room was
warming up.

Patty, Norm, and Sharry were organizing
and unloading the food delivery.

Sam handed me some of the equipment
I had requested. I thanked him and

disappeared into the freezer. Miro resumed her post at the doorway.

I immediately drew a sketch of everything I saw, noting distances between the body and landmarks, such as the drain, the doorway, and the nearest freezer shelves.

I slapped on some latex gloves and dove into my kit bag for my tools. Tried and true, they had been collected over the years with the help of my mentor in the department. Juan Antonio was the best the department had ever seen. He was amazing at interviewing witnesses and the best in the interrogation room. I had stood behind the two-way mirror many times to hear him in action and learn from him.

I used a pair of tweezers from my evidence kit to remove the black hair on Olive's shirt. I carefully placed it in a paper towel and rolled it up several times. I labeled a paper bag with the date and the time.

I looked at the note, holding one corner of it with tweezers.

"I don't think I can really lift good prints off of this one, Miro," I said. "Maybe the lab will be able to get something." I placed the note in a paper bag. I did the same with the grocery list. I put the aspirin in a small, clean jar and labeled it with masking tape.

The wadded tissue and the small amount of blood on Olive's body could be analyzed in the lab. DNA tests could be done to follow up on my preliminary work.

The gritty substance was scooped up with the side of a sheet of paper. I dropped it into an envelope that I had already labeled. I did the same with the white substance.

I used a sharp knife supplied by Sam to scrape up the frozen puddle that was close to the body. I dropped it into a glass jar and sealed the lid tightly.

I put each item in its own brown paper wrapping and then placed them in a box. I labeled the box with a list of the items. I surveyed the scene again, hoping to notice something new. I left everything as it was. Even the fallen cabbages.

"Olive Souffle," I said, "I will find out who killed you and why. I owe you a favor." With that Miro and I left the freezer and sealed it shut.

In the kitchen, Caesar had started coffee on the gas stove and it smelled wonderful. I settled into a chair at the long counter where I could see the freezer.

I thought about breakfast. Miro looked hungry, too, and I asked if there was something for her to eat. Caesar was happy to oblige, and pretty soon Miro was smacking her chops on a huge cooking bone.

"Why didn't you put everything into one container with a larger label?" asked Patty, peering at the evidence I had put on the counter. She had finished her work with Norm and Sharry and was settling down in front of me at the counter with a cup of coffee.

"Good question," I said. "What happens if you seal a piece of pie in plastic wrap and leave it on the counter for days on end?"

"It spoils," Patty said.

"Right," I agreed. "The mold that grows on it makes in inedible. Well, if I put evidence samples into plastic containers and sealed them airtight, I'd be setting up the same situation. Bacteria and mold love anaerobic, or low oxygen, areas that are warm and humid."

"So what did you put everything in?" Norm asked. He had been trying the phone, with no luck, and now had come over to join us.

"I put everything in paper bags sealed with tape and ID stickers," I said. "The paper lets the samples breathe."

Patty and Norm seemed to lose interest in my lecture on crime science. Patty drifted over to a high counter and started to scan a notebook filled with recipes. Norm took off outside. I could see him talking with Sharry, who was shoveling snow off the steps.

Around me, the kitchen bustled with life. A battery-powered radio was playing upbeat tunes. Caesar had started slicing onions and the pungent odor drifted to the table. I watched his thick arms move nimbly over the cutting board, his fingers a blur of action as they diced three green peppers into perfect squares. I tried my hardest not to drool when I smelled the mouth-watering aroma of frying onions in a spicy olive oil and watched him make a perfect omelette. I was hungry, I'll admit it.

Caesar is strong yet precise, I thought as I watched him work. He was capable of doing some serious damage with his muscular bulk. Was he a murderer?

It was important to test the evidence as soon as possible in case it got tampered with while I was away or if something degraded chemically.

"Sharry," I called out to her from the service door entrance.

"Yeah, Cardoni. What's up?" she said.

"I was wondering if you could fix me up with a new lock and a key?" I asked politely.

"A good idea," she said as if reading my mind. "I can get you a new one with a single key, right out of the box."

"Appreciate that, Sharry," I said.

I went back to my little work area. I had pretty much what I needed to conduct my tests. I had three extra emergency candles in case I worked later than daylight.

"What are you doing?" Caesar asked as he ate his omelette.

"I'm sterilizing the counter with diluted bleach. I won't have an appetite after catching a whiff of this stuff," I answered.

He looked at me closely. "How do you do it?" he asked. "You know—deal with dead bodies?"

"I think of it as a story," I said. "The murder is the way the story starts out. My job is to write the ending. I need to piece together each victim's story so that justice wins in the end."

He nodded his head again approvingly, put his plate and fork into the sink, then returned to his area.

I returned to my work. I had to figure out the chemical properties of the substances I had found at the scene.

The white crystal substance I had recovered near Olive Souffle's head was intriguing. I looked at it with a magnifying lens. I opened up a notebook I keep with me all the time. At the top of one page, I wrote the date and Olive's name. Then I jotted down, *white substance: definitely crystalline shape, solid*. I sniffed it by waving my hand over it, indirectly wafting any fumes to my nose. No distinct odor.

Thanks to the gas stoves, I could heat up substances. I grabbed the coat hanger that

Sharry had brought me. I unwound the neck of the hanger and turned it into a long metal stick, something like a marshmallow roaster.

"Isn't it a little early in the day for marsh-mallows?" asked Walter, amused at my handiwork.

He had snuck up on me. I wanted to yell at him but this was not my turf. He had a spiral notebook in his right hand and was taking notes, too. I had no idea what he was writing, but it annoyed the heck out of me.

"We've got plenty of shish kabob shewers, if you want one," Sam added helpfully from his area across the room.

"No, thanks. I'm fine with what I've got going right here," I said as I concentrated.

Sam went back to doing his work.

Walter smiled at me as if I were a child and took a step closer to the stove, notebook poised, ready to record every move I made.

"I'm going to need to concentrate here, so if you don't mind . . ." I said. Walter got the hint. He left to go write up someone else.

I reached into my bag and pulled out some nichrome wire, a handy combination of nickel and chrome that's soft and pliable. I unrolled a small section, snipped it with pliers and formed a small loop at one end. I attached the other end to the coat hanger. Basically, I had constructed an extension of the coat hanger.

Turning on the stove, I placed a few crystals of the white substance on the tiny looped end of the nichrome wire and held it in the flame.

I was surprised at what happened. When I held it very close to the flame, the white crystals burned a sickly black as if rotting instantly. I couldn't smell anything until I removed it from the flame. I knew I was going to remember this smell.

Walter's smirking face came into view as he peered over the side of the counter to check my work.

"What are you doing?" he asked with great interest.

"Working," I replied.

"Fine, see if I care," he said airily and slouched off.

Okay, I thought. *Maybe he has something to hide.* I turned to a clean page in my notebook. I put Walter's name at the top of the page, then I wrote *What a pest! Curious— or worried about the results?*

"May I?" a voice asked. It was Sam.

I nodded.

He sat down on a stool in front of me. His long hair was pulled back into a ponytail. His tie-dyed shirt was definitely a statement. He looked at me suddenly, as if he had read my thoughts. Then he smiled.

I made a mental note to write down, *Sam.*

Has a sweet smile.

"What exactly are you doing?" he asked.

"I'm doing a flame test," I answered.

"A what?" he asked, interested.

"I'm trying to figure out what the evidence is by the color it gives off when it burns in this flame," I explained.

"How does that work?" he asked.

"See the fire in the fireplace?" I asked.

He glanced at it as if seeing it for the first time, then nodded.

"The colors in the flame are due to the materials being burned as well as the chemicals that are in the air," I explained. "Chemicals such as nitrogen, a small bit of argon, carbon dioxide, some other gases, and what we rely on to breathe—oxygen."

Sam nodded again. He was with me so far.

"The flames in the fire are different from the flames on the gas stove, aren't they?" I directed him to look.

"Why, so they are!" he exclaimed softly.

The gas flames were a bright-looking blue with an occasional orange flash when the flame burned a discarded morsel of food on the grill.

"What colors do you see in the candle flame right here?" I asked as I lit the emergency candle.

"Yellow at the tip to a darker orange toward the base and a dark blue right at the bottom. It seems more like the fire flame," he said, glancing at the fireplace.

"Good observation," I said approvingly.

"Each of those colors means a different component of air burning?" He seemed pleased with the new information.

"It also indicates the temperature of the burning," I added. "The shape, size, and precise colors depend on the temperature of the surroundings, the size of the wick, even the fuel source. Regardless of these minor details, you'll always be able to tell a candle flame from a gas stove flame."

I lifted the nichrome wire close to his face so he could see it. Then it dawned on him.

"So if you burn a substance in a flame, it will burn a certain color?" he asked.

"One color if it's an element. Several different colors if there's a mixture or a compound involved."

"So what is the white crystal stuff?" he asked as he craned to read my notes.

"It's surprisingly nontoxic and easy to obtain," I said as I placed another bit on the end of the nichrome wire loop.

He smiled when he saw the result. The familiar caramelizing effect was not hard for a dessert chef to recognize. The smell of burnt raisins wafted through the air for a brief second as the sample burned quickly.

"That's sugar!" he exclaimed.

"The question is, what is sugar doing in a freezer near the head of a dead chef?" I asked, more to myself than to anyone else.

6

Breakfast
a la Carte

"**S**AM!" a voice yelled from across the room.

"Wha . . .?" he asked, turning to see what the problem was.

"Ohmigosh!" he exclaimed as he dashed to his counter. The oven was merciless. He had left a cake to brown and it had gotten a good scorching.

I made a new page for Sam in my notebook. *Seems like a nice guy. Bright, curious, but sometimes forgetful.*

"We must seem like a dysfunctional family to you," Sam said as he scraped away the burned pieces from the top of the cake.

"Don't know yet," I said, embarrassed that he had noticed my studying him. *Perceptive*, I added in my notebook.

I looked at my watch. It was 8:20 A.M. I looked to the outside. Sharry was stomping snow off her boots at the service door entrance. My stomach was growling again and I was determined to have breakfast before I continued. I wrote down the results of the flame test: *sugar.*

Sharry brought me a brand new heavy-duty lock and a set of keys. I sealed the freezer door and hoped that no one would be able to foil the lock. Miro looked on approvingly as I installed it with Sharry's help. I returned to the counter where my tests sat, waiting for me to finish.

Walter joined me. I just couldn't seem to shake the guy. He was a serious showman, very smooth. I could imagine him greeting his rich resort guests with so much greasy charm they might slip down the stairs.

Walter noticed Miro.

"Does the *dog* have to be here?" he asked.

"She does," I said.

"Fine," he said, "when she makes a mess you'll have to clean it up."

I was disgusted. Miro was well-trained, which was obvious to everyone else in the room except Walter. I made a quick note on my Walter page: *Allergies? Scared of Miro?*

The sound of a chair scraping the floor made me look up suddenly. Sharry had taken the seat at the opposite end of the table. She sipped her coffee slowly, cradling the mug in her hands, elbows on the table. It looked like her special ritual, one not to be interrupted by conversation.

Her thick mane of brown hair was slicked with sweat from her exercise outdoors. Her sweaters were piled up by the fireplace to dry out. She sat quietly, listening to the others.

I made a few notes in my notebook. *Sharry. Seems to take everything in stride, as if a murder is a common occurrence. If she's disturbed by the events of the morning, she's doing a great job disguising it.*

Patty had joined the group. She was dressed smartly in a sweater and heavy boots. Her hair was brushed back into a bun, neater than earlier this morning. I noticed the earrings in her left ear, sparkling in the pale morning light. She was composed and her face had lost the puffy redness from crying.

I wrote, *Patty. Alert, confident.*

Norm had lost the funky hat and had on an old sweatshirt over jeans. His boots looked used and abused and very comfortable. He sat down next to Patty. I wrote, *Are Patty and Norm an item?*

With a theatrical flourish, Caesar presented omelettes to everyone seated at the table. Dishes and silverware clinked as people started breakfast. The popping and crackling of the fire in the fireplace was a steady, soothing backdrop.

It was strange. The kitchen was warm,

almost inviting. If I hadn't known it was a murder scene, I'd swear it was the most friendly atmosphere I had ever experienced.

"So when do you think the medical examiner will get here, Cardoni?" Norm asked. They all turned to look at me.

"I spoke with their office and they expect him to be here after two this afternoon. Of course, that depends on the state of the roads," I said.

Everyone seemed to take this information in stride, as if discussing the arrival of the medical examiner were an everyday occurrence. The conversation shifted and focused on the opening of the resort in two days, their concerns for the menu, the delivery of all the necessary supplies.

". . . join us?" someone was asking.

"Pardon?" I said, focusing.

"Would you like to join us and sample some of Caesar's award-winning omelettes?" Walter asked.

I was ready to walk over. I looked at their expectant faces. What if the murderer were still around and didn't like my investigation? What if one of them had poisoned food intended for me? What if *all* of them had poisoned food intended for me? My stomach growled so loudly that I was sure they would hear it.

7

Basically Sam

"**I** DON'T HAVE MUCH of an appetite now," I said pleasantly. I was lying. I could have eaten a bear. I went back to jotting down notes as I listened to the conversation. Breakfast was soon over.

I looked at my watch. It was 9:30 A.M. The dishes had been cleared and loaded into an industrial dishwasher. Patty walked off to check stock in one of the refrigerators. Norm sat by the fireplace reading an old newspaper. Walter was immersed in a recipe book at Caesar's desk. Sam was hard at work at his counter. Caesar had cleaned up his work area and was puttering around, opening and closing drawers.

I devoured a few sports bars I kept in my bag. I washed them down with a can of soda. I looked outside. It had stopped snowing much earlier in the morning. What remained was a beautiful blanket of white. The fir tree branches bowed from their weight. I could see Sharry back outside shoveling snow by the entrance to the garage, just to the right of the service door. I could see her with her sunglasses and wild patterned hat.

The road was nowhere near being cleared. I hadn't seen or heard a snowplow all morning, I realized. It would be a while before Dr. Lawson arrived. I had survived breakfast, though. And I was forming a game plan for the case.

"So Angel, what do you think?" Sam asked from his counter. He held up an incredible-looking pastry confection. It was a snowman made of chocolate and coconut.

"Nice," I said, walking over to admire his artistry. The counter was littered with waxed paper, chocolate shavings, coconut morsels, sugar, and flour. I had noticed that he had called me by my first name, and I had to admit that was nice, too.

"You know what?" I said. "It smells like a chocolate store in here. The odors literally attack your sense of smell. At work we call them chocolate muggings. Sergeants use them on officers to get in good or to apologize for messing up."

Sam laughed. "I'll have to call my next creation a chocolate mugging."

I inhaled deeply.

"Did you know that without your sense of smell, you can easily lose all appetite?"

Sam asked.

"Really? Well, that would seem logical. We derive our sense of taste from our sense of smell." I remembered being sick with a cold and not being interested in food for a week.

"Would you like to try it?" Sam asked as he held up a fork.

Would I.

"Thanks, it looks incredible, but I'm avoiding sweets." I was lying again. Better to drool over chocolate I can't have than to be dead from just one little taste.

"Suit yourself," Sam said, not sounding the least bit offended. He busied himself with the recipe book, noting changes in his ingredients. The pages had chocolate and candy-colored splatters. It was obviously a well-used book.

Miro had wandered over and her large watery eyes turned on the familiar begging look.

"Your dog's pretty cool," Sam said as he grabbed a chunk of chocolate from the box.

Miro looked delighted with the prospect of a snack.

"Please don't feed that to her," I said quickly.

"Why? It's not poisoned or anything," Sam said.

"Chocolate can kill a dog," I said. I pointed to Miro and then indicated a corner of the room. Dejected, she wandered away, her claws clicking on the floor.

"Didn't know that," Sam said. "Sorry."

"No harm done."

"So what do you think about Olive?" Sam asked.

"You mean have I figured out who killed her?" I answered.

"Basically," he said.

"Not yet. Since you brought it up, do you mind if I ask you where you were last night between 12:40 and 6:00 this morning?"

"I'm a suspect?" he asked.

"No, I just need to know everyone's whereabouts, to get an idea of what might have happened," I said as I shrugged my shoulders.

"So I'm a suspect," he repeated.

"Basically," I shot back.

"What time did she die?" he asked, steering the conversation.

I spouted off Dr. Lawson's time-of-death speech. "If you weren't with the person when he or she died, you cannot state a time of death. If you know exactly when, then I'd probably guess that you're an accessory to murder."

"What *do* you know?" he asked pointedly.

"Estimated time of death is somewhere between 12:40 and 6:00 A.M.," I said.

"Do you think one of us did it?" His voice

was hushed, as if he didn't want the walls to hear our conversation.

I looked around. We were alone in the kitchen.

"I need facts before I can think about who did it or how," I said.

"What's the medical examiner going to do?" he asked.

"He'll examine the body and try to give me an opinion on the nature and cause of death."

"Wasn't she stabbed?" he asked as he turned to sculpting another chocolate confection.

"How do you know?" I asked.

"Norm told me," he said matter-of-factly.

"How does Norm know?" I retorted.

"He saw the body in the freezer," he finished. "I also noticed that you didn't eat any omelettes for breakfast. Are you worried one of us would poison you?" He took out a mixing bowl and measured out two cups of icing sugar.

"Maybe I'm a strict vegetarian," I said, growing impatient with the sudden amateur sleuthing.

"Really? Hey, so am I." His tone softened. He added butter to the sugar and began mashing the mixture together with a wooden spoon. He added a tiny amount of water and mixed the ingredients together into a smooth paste. Then he added a drop of red food coloring to the bowl and I watched, mesmerized as it bled into the mixture.

"So, Sam," I said as he stirred, "what were you doing last night?"

"I was sleeping, Cardoni. Plain and simple." With that the conversation ended abruptly. On a last-name basis, I noticed.

Right. Okay. Back to my corner of the kitchen where I was down for the count.

All of a sudden, there were three ear-splitting explosions that rang in my ears: *Bang! Bang! Bang!* Then silence.

8

A Motive
for Murder?

"CARDONI! Cardoni!" Someone was shouting my name.

Miro was barking furiously. I looked outside. It was Bert banging on the windows. He waved to me to come outside.

I cleared up my clutter and bundled into my extra sweater and jacket. Waiting outside was none other than shopkeeper-turned-informant, Bert Paltry.

"So, Cardoni, wha'd'ya think? Huh? Wha'd'ya think? Huh?"

I groaned inwardly. There was no escape.

"I can tell you've got some good information for me," I said in my best deadpan.

"You bet your badge I do," he said triumphantly. He hopped ahead of us, leading the way to the road. Sharry looked at us from inside the cab of the lodge's snowplow and shook her head.

What was I getting myself into?

Bert made a sharp right between the lodge and the garage. He looked back, waiting impatiently. I reached for my shades. It was glaringly sunny outside. Miro was sniffing around an oak overburdened by snow.

"Just where are we going, Bert?" I asked as I caught up to him. I stepped onto the snowbank and promptly sank up to my knees.

"Here, put these on," he said as he handed me an extra pair of snowshoes that were propped up against a tree. The man was prepared. I was impressed.

I fastened them on. Miro looked around confused, like, *where's my pair?*

"C'm'ere girl!" I called.

She plowed up the embankment and immediately sank to her chest. I followed Bert and Miro followed in our tracks.

"Seriously Bert, where are we going?"

"I'm going to show you a motive for murder," he said, trying not to sound excited but failing terribly.

"A motive for who?" I asked.

"You'll see when we get there," he said.

Miro came up for air. She developed a rhythm of diving and resurfacing like a dolphin. She was panting furiously, her breath a sudden wet rain in the cold air.

"Here it is," Bert announced.

He stood aside for me to glimpse the big secret that was going to crack this case wide open.

A rusted chain-link fence blocked our path. It stood in front of a black, yawning opening in the side of a hill. It was covered in snow, almost natural-looking despite the fence. It was the opening to a mine.

"Okay?" I said. "What's the deal here?"

"So, what do you think is cool about this mine?" Bert pressed me to guess.

"It's full of gold?" I ventured.

"Close," he said. "Do you still have my cell phone?"

"Yes."

"Call the County Records Clerk. Ask who owns this land."

I did. Just as soon as we got back inside.

"County Records," a voice said.

"Hello, I wou . . ."

"If you would like to speak to the clerk, please press one. If you would like to speak to the secretary, please press two. If you would like to speak to anyone else, please remain on the line and an operator will assist you shortly."

Ah, the universal answering machine. Technology had invaded the quiet country-side.

"Well? Huh?" Bert was impatient.

"County Records."

"This is Detective Cardoni. Badge number 3299. I'm working a murder investigation. I'm looking for the name of the owner of an abandoned mine in Bear County."

"That would be the abandoned gold mine two miles southeast of Bear Lodge?"

"Wow, yes, that's it."

"Don't be impressed. It's the only mine in the tri-county area," the voice said.

"I'd like to know who currently owns it. And the lodge," I added hastily, on impulse.

Paper shuffling.

"Computers down?" I said, doing the conversational thing.

"Power's out. We have paper files, too. It'll take just a sec, here. Lot number 000-086432 belongs to Paris Peace."

Peace? As in Walter?

"Thank you very much for your time," I said and hung up.

"So...whad-I-tell-ya, huh?" Bert asked eagerly.

"Who do you think owns the land, Bert?" I asked him.

"Olive Souffle, huh?" he said, confidently.

"Why do you think that?" I asked.

"Because the previous owner was going to sell it to her and . . . huh." He sounded less certain of himself.

"Who told you?" I probed.

"Olive did, just a few weeks ago. Huh.

We were having coffee. She beat me three straight games of checkers," he said without shame.

"Did she say who the previous owner was?" I pressed.

"No, huh," he admitted. "But she said the previous owner's son wanted to develop it into a tourist place—you know, water rides and a bunch of other stuff. Olive wanted to see it preserved as a nature retreat."

"Did anybody else hear your conversation?"

"Not that I know of, huh," he said slowly.

A group of crows had gathered in the trees above us. Perhaps they had spotted something tasty in the snow. One by one, they slowly came to the ground, black blobs against a white setting.

A blinding flash of recall hit me. I thought back to Olive Souffle's grocery list. The word *pois*, the French word for "peas" had been circled.

Had Olive been trying to give us a clue?

9

What Is
That Red Stuff?

IT WAS 10:20 A.M. when we returned to the lodge. I waved absentmindedly as Bert headed back to his store to wait for the roads to clear. My mind had shifted into high gear. As I hiked back to the lodge, I looked around, but didn't really see the landscape. I saw motives, a kitchen full of suspects, and the murder of a great chef.

I took off my snowshoes once I reached the driveway. Sharry had cleared a huge area for parking. Miro was at full gallop on hard snow, her tongue lolling out. Exhausted as she was, this whole hike had been a great experience for her.

"Miro, let's scare up something to eat, huh?"

Whoa. Enough hanging out with Bert-huh-Paltry.

I shook the snow off my boots and socks,

stomping on the rubber matting of the service door entrance. Miro promptly lay down. Break time. My jacket was warm and sweaty. I hung it up by the fire. I scarfed down another sports bar and got ready for work.

I needed facts, information. A little creativity and science would put me in business. Back to the tests. But I was limited to what I could do in a kitchen during a power failure.

Norm had returned to his newspaper by the fire. He got up periodically to check to see if the phone was working. With his busy delivery schedule, I was sure that he had other customers waiting farther down the road. His hulking form was strangely out of place in the kitchen and he seemed to be aware of it.

Sam was still working in earnest on his pastries. He waved his knife as though it were a magic wand as he iced his confections. I could barely hear him humming to himself over the racket in the kitchen. His whole body seemed intent upon the work. He seemed so focused.

Caesar was talking to himself softly. He seemed preoccupied, picking up different kitchen tools and moving others in their drawers. I guessed he was doing an inventory of sorts.

I reached into my evidence box and pulled out a vial of red liquid. *Where did this come from?* It was the bottle that I had labeled from the freezer. I remembered scraping up a clear solid. Obviously, the solid had melted when I took the vial out of the freezer. But how did it get to be red?

"Something's definitely wrong here," I muttered. The clear liquid was far enough away from the spot of blood that I had seen near the opening of Olive's shirt. I was sure I hadn't mixed the two together when I took the samples.

I looked around the kitchen while everyone bustled about. I was lost in thought. Maybe it was red when I originally picked it up. No, that couldn't be it. Maybe it got contaminated after I put it in the jar and sealed it.

I began to write in my notebook. *Sam handed me a knife. I scraped a portion into the jar and sealed it tight. Maybe someone tampered with the evidence during breakfast. No, it couldn't have been disturbed when I was around. I sealed the jar! The redness simply must have been there originally. I must not have noticed it.*

Nothing really made sense. I would have to run some chemical tests to see what the most logical explanation was.

The coolest thing about all substances is

that they each have unique identifying fingerprints. A substance has its own boiling point, melting and freezing point, and density. I would run a boiling point test and then follow up with a density and a pH test to confirm the results.

I would need a few more simple materials. I walked over to Caesar. He was still rummaging through the drawers when he wasn't stirring up a storm in the soup pot.

"Caesar, I was wondering if I could borrow one of your thermometers?" I asked politely.

"What kind do you need?" he asked.

"Do you have a digital thermometer?" I asked. I figured it couldn't hurt to ask for a precise measuring device.

"Not a problem," Caesar said as he turned to a drawer and pulled out a shiny black-and-silver-colored model. It was nestled in a drawer with several other types of thermometers, all neatly organized.

"Thank you so much," I said. "I promise to return it before the end of the day."

As I walked away, I felt waves of negative energy coming from him, the kind that make you shudder. I reminded myself to add this observation to my notes.

I also needed a small pot of some sort. I looked at Sam. He was smiling at me as if to say, "Yes? What do you need?"

"Sam," I said as I approached his counter,

"would you be so kind as to let me borrow a small pot?" I paused.

"Certainly," he said as he offered a smaller, delicate saucepan. It was sparkling clean.

"Thank you."

Miro stretched as I returned. She looked at me drowsily and groaned as she fell back asleep.

I placed a small quantity of the red liquid into the saucepan. I looked at the tip of the probe of the thermometer. The end was spotless, as if it had hardly been used.

I set the saucepan on the stovetop and turned on the gas. I rested the probe of the thermometer in the red liquid and not on the bottom of the pan. Doing so would have given me the temperature of the metal pan as it warmed up, which would have been much hotter than the liquid.

I didn't notice anything strange about the liquid as it heated. There were no odors, no chemical changes. It didn't take long to heat to boiling. I watched the digital display creep up slowly. When it reached about 80 degrees Celsius, I noticed a few bubbles here and there that seemed to come from the pan itself. Between 99 and 100 degrees Celsius, the liquid was boiling steadily. Okay. So the boiling point of the liquid was 100 degrees Celsius. I knew of one substance that boiled at that temperature. I was puzzled and not yet convinced of my findings. I wrote down: *boiling point, 100 degrees Celsius.*

I turned off the stove and looked at the red liquid that remained in the jar. I would perform a density test next.

I walked over to Patty's area. "What is it?" she asked stiffly.

"I was wondering if you would be so kind as to lend me some equipment?" I asked.

"What kind of test can you run with them?" she asked, hostile as a little sister who has to share toys.

"If you could loan me a narrow, cylindrical container to measure a quantity of a liquid and a small scale to measure its mass, I could calculate density."

She looked in a drawer and pulled out what looked like a hypodermic needle.

"I use it for injecting spices in tarts or sweetened syrup into chocolate or other desserts," she said.

The needle seemed very threatening in her hands. I thanked her for it while she bent over, digging into a drawer for something.

"You'll also find this scale most useful," she said as she presented it to me. Would I ever! It was a battery-powered digital scale with measurements in grams.

"Thank you."

I walked over to my work area and felt Patty's eyes boring two holes in my back.

The hairs stood up on my neck.

I looked at the evidence box. I still had so many more tests to do before I could propose any sort of modus operandi—how the murder was committed. I needed to get back to work.

I found the mass of the empty hypodermic needle and jotted down the information in my notebook. I would fill the needle with 5 milliliters of the red liquid and then determine *its* mass. I carefully filled the reservoir to 5 ml by knocking out a few air bubbles and then rested the needle on the balance.

That was funny. The mass of the liquid alone was precisely 5 grams. I tried again, resetting the balance to zero to make sure everything was right. It was. Well, the ratio of mass to volume meant that the liquid's density was 1 *gram per milliliter.* It couldn't be! Otherwise it could only be one substance. I would run one more test on it just to be sure.

I approached the freezer and unlocked it. Miro had followed and she obediently sat by the door as I went in to retrieve a cabbage. It was more than just freezing cold in there. It was ominous. It felt like the county morgue—cold, sterile, and deathly, isolated from any living being. I felt so sorry for Olive. She was one of the few victims I had actually met and known, however briefly, before she was killed. I grabbed a cabbage and left, sealing the door behind me.

Miro whined softly, as if she understood my thoughts and was trying to comfort and encourage me.

I gathered a wooden chopping board and a sharp knife. The other chefs looked at me in amusement. I found an old apron in the drawer at my station and put it on.

Walter could not resist. "Applying for a job here, are we?"

"There is an opening now that Olive's gone," Caesar said slowly from his area.

Sam glanced up with a faraway look in his eyes. I couldn't tell if he was lost in the music of his radio or if he was thinking about Olive.

Miro settled on the floor at the end of the counter, her large, liquid eyes filled with concern. She had seen and tasted many of my attempts at cooking. She did not look thrilled that she might have to do it again.

I scribbled in my notebook. *Confirm my suspicions . . . is red liquid an acid, base—or is it neutral?*

I put a pot of water on the stove and set the gas to high, hoping to get a rolling boil. I placed the cabbage on the cutting board and made a hacking cut that split it in half. Caesar was looking long and hard at me. Patty had looked up and couldn't seem to look away. Even Sam was distracted.

I ignored everyone as best as I could and proceeded to chop the cabbage into slivers. I scooped the slivers into the bubbling distilled water and lowered the heat. It simmered for about twenty minutes while I carefully stirred. By this time I had Caesar, Sharry, and Patty sitting at my counter. How could I comfortably explain to a group of potential suspects the methods I was using to catch the killer?

"What in the world are you doing?" Walter asked as he joined the group, pen in hand, ready to take notes.

"Just preparing a stock solution of a chemical indicator," I replied.

"A red cabbage is a chemical indicator?" scoffed Caesar.

"Yes," I said, "especially when it is combined with the test substances."

They watched as the water turned a mysterious purple and the cabbages seemed to lose their color. I turned the heat off. With the help of a cooking mitt, I poured the contents of the pot through a sieve and into a clean glass bowl.

I discarded the remaining leaves and labeled five different drinking glasses with masking tape and a marker. I recognized a distracting colorful presence out of the corner of my eye.

"Now what are you going to do?" Sam asked. A buzzer went off from a corner of the kitchen and Caesar disappeared to attend to his work.

"I'll show you how easy it is to figure out how acidic or basic a substance is," I said as I hunted around the drawers for something to test besides the red liquid.

"Does anyone here have a lemon or lemonade?" I asked.

"Lemonade in the second refrigerator," Patty said as she got up to get some.

"Great, thanks. How about some window cleaner or straight-up ammonia?" I asked Sharry.

"Fourth cabinet to your left," she indicated.

"And some more distilled water," I said and filled a glass.

Patty returned with the lemonade.

"Anybody have baking soda?" I asked.

Sam broke away from the group and returned with a small square box.

I finally had assembled the four test solutions along with the red liquid. Into each glass I poured about 20 ml of the dark, reddish-purple liquid. I then added about 5 ml of the substances I wished to test into their respective glasses. The chefs seemed impressed. It was so elementary, but it looked good.

"The indicator is simply going to tell me if the liquid I scooped up in the freezer is an acid, a base, or neutral," I said quietly, as I concentrated on the task at hand.

The distilled water remained the dark, reddish-purple color. There was essentially no change. The lemonade had changed color to a beautiful blood-red, almost a crimson. On the other hand, the ammonia changed the indicator to a deep pine green. The baking soda turned it a dark blue, putting it on the side of basic but not as strong a base as the ammonia.

They all seemed to expect something dramatic from the red liquid, so when the indicator experienced no color change, they seemed disappointed.

"What does that mean?" Sam asked, as he nodded toward the last glass.

"It means that we have a neutral substance," I said.

"The red liquid that you found is neutral?" asked Walter. His brows were knitted in a frown and he gave off bad vibes.

"Isn't blood neutral?" Norm offered from his position, hanging onto the group from the end.

"Yes, blood is more neutral at a pH of around 7.4," I agreed. "But this red liquid has a boiling point of 100 degrees Celsius and a density of 1.0 grams per ml."

"So what is it?" asked Sharry, as she took a sip of her water.

"The same stuff you're drinking," I said.

10

Nothing on Norm

"SAY WHAT?" Sharry said, nearly spraying water all over the kitchen.

"The red liquid is water," I stated flatly.

"How does it fit into the crime?" Walter asked. He seemed genuinely interested.

"It could be melted snow that was left in the freezer and eventually froze," I guessed.

"Why is it red?" asked Sam.

"My question exactly. That's what I'm here to find out."

Everone looked at everyone else and seemed to agree that I was not up to this job.

Our little seminar group seemed to split up rather quickly. I was left with Miro looking up at me expectantly. Did she have to try my newest creation?

"No, Miro. You don't have to sweat it this time," I said as I patted her head and scratched behind her ears, something she loves.

I was puzzled. Sam had gotten to the crux

of the situation. If it was water and it was clear when I had first seen it, and if I hadn't contaminated it in its container, what happened, then?

I wrote in my notebook in huge letters. *Why did the clear liquid turn red and when?* I underlined that last word about twenty times.

I looked around at my suspects. If the murder of Olive Souffle had been a conspiracy, it meant that everyone knew about it. Someone was probably busting with the secret. That's a hard burden to bear. I've seen criminals turn informant in the middle of an interrogation because they just wanted to tell someone, never mind shorten their jail time. I scribbled, *conspiracy*? I added about twenty question marks.

At this rate, I was going to have to get a new notebook.

Who could I get to first? I wondered.

Norm wandered into the kitchen through the lobby entrance and grabbed a pitcher of orange juice out of the refrigerator. I watched him as he took a long swig.

He looked around the kitchen. His eyes rested on me.

I smiled.

"Hi, Norm. If you have a few minutes, I'd really appreciate your help with something," I said as I frowned at the equipment in front of me. I hoped I was looking lost and in need of help.

"Pretty cool dog," Norm said as he slowly walked over.

"She sure is," I said as I wiped down the counter.

"Does she bite?" he asked.

"Miro? Do you bite?" I asked her. Upon hearing her name, Miro lifted her head suddenly.

"C'm'ere girl," I said as I patted my thigh.

She stretched and came to sit between us. Norm offered his hand for her to sniff. Miro obliged, then she let him pet her, her eyes not leaving him.

"It must have been pretty scary finding Olive's body," I said suddenly.

"Yeah, it was," he readily agreed.

"Patty seemed pretty shook up," I ventured.

"Yeah, she sure was," Norm said as he stood back and looked at Miro.

He looked over the counter at the kitchen utensils, the paper and plastic containers scattered everywhere.

"I was just wondering what time you got here?" I asked as I puttered around, fussing with nothing in particular.

"A little before 6:00 this morning," he answered quickly. I jotted this down while he looked at Miro.

"Patty was already up and about?" I asked.

"Yeah," he said.

"Where did you come in?" I asked casually.

"The service door," he said. *Service door*, I wrote.

"Did you knock?" I quizzed.

"No, Patty was there. She let me in," he answered abruptly.

"Did you talk about anything or did you immediately begin delivering the cabbages?"

"She offered me some coffee. It was cold out," he explained.

"Did you have coffee before you delivered the first load?" I asked.

"No, I already had the dolly loaded up and I wheeled it over to the freezer," he explained.

"What was on the dolly?" I asked.

"Produce, stuff like that," he said. "You remember, the cabbages fell down."

"Oh right," I said slowly, as if I didn't remember.

"Yeah, we walked in and almost tripped over Olive Souffle's body!" he exclaimed.

"Did you touch her?" I asked. "Did you move the body?"

"I checked for a pulse on her wrist, but that was it," he said.

"Did Patty touch the body?" I asked.

"No, she just screamed," he replied.

"Then what happened after you checked for a pulse?" I persisted.

"You showed up!" he exclaimed.

"Do you know if Olive had any enemies?" I quizzed.

"She was pretty stuck up," he began, "but, no, I don't know."

"Ever hear anyone threaten her?"

"No," he replied.

"How about arguments or fights among the chefs or the staff?"

"No."

"Well, thanks Norm. I appreciate the information," I said as I turned my attention to the evidence in front of me. *Norm* and *nothing* were the only two words I wrote in my notebook.

Just then, the wall phone rang, and we all jumped. Finally—the phones were working! Norm scurried to answer it. "Cardoni, it's for you," he said gruffly, as if he had just lost a popularity contest.

"This is Cardoni," I began.

"Well, hello!" A friendly voice at the other end warmed my heart. It was Dr. Lawson, the medical examiner. "How are you holding up, Cardoni?" he asked.

"Hangin' in there," I said, aware that everyone in the room was listening.

"Listen, can I call you back on another phone?" I asked.

"Not a problem," he said.

I got his number and called him immediately from another phone in the corner of the kitchen. The chefs got the message. Most left the room. We wouldn't be overheard.

"Where are you?" I asked.

"We're stuck in a rustic and quaint little town called Witches' Gulf," he said. "The road should be cleared in another hour or so. So what's going on?" he asked.

"I'm surrounded by murderous chefs, all bent on finishing me in some culinary death," I replied, trying to joke.

Miro walked over and plopped down at my feet, one paw resting possessively on my boots.

"Don, you'd better get here as soon as you can," I said.

"What's the problem—I mean, besides the bunch of murderous chefs?" he asked lightly.

"I'm getting the weirdest results from the tests I'm performing," I answered.

"What have you done already?" he inquired.

I gave him a brief update and he uh-huhed attentively.

I looked around the kitchen to Sam. He was icing another one of his confections with his long, slender fingers. The knife held a dollop of red icing.

"I'm just not clear where the . . . red . . .

comes . . . from." I hesitated, making a connection. It came to me in a blinding flash.

"Don, you have probably never seen this kind of a murder weapon," I said quickly.

"What do you mean? I thought you were talking about some physical evidence. Where is the murder weapon?" he asked patiently.

"It's the red liquid," I said.

"Huh?"

"Listen. I can't talk now," I said quickly. "I really have to go."

"*Cardoni!*" he shouted into the phone.

"Yeah?"

"Be careful."

11

What Is
That Gritty Stuff?

I LOOKED AT my watch: 12:15 P.M. With renewed vigor, I attacked my next series of tests. Dr. Lawson was on his way. Help was coming. I nearly sang the words.

I cleared up my work area and pulled out the clean spice jar that held the gritty substance. The grains spilled against the sides of the container. Caught by the sunlight, a few even sparkled as they moved. I reached into my kit and grabbed a magnifying glass.

I could make out the different sizes, shapes, and colors of the grains in the jar. I wrote a description of what I saw: *Mixture of tiny solid grains of different shades of brown, black, and gray.*

I poured a small portion onto a coffee filter. I used a spoon to smooth the mound flat. The crystal-like solid grains scratched against the metal of the spoon.

I heated up about 500 ml of distilled water in a clean pan. The water didn't need to boil, only simmer. I found a small funnel and lined it with the coffee filter paper. I transferred the warm water to a glass bowl and added about a teaspoonful of the gritty substance. I stirred it slowly, watching carefully as tiny jet streams of brown and black particles swirled around the spoon.

Still stirring, I slowly poured the mixture into the funnel, a bit at a time. I didn't want it to splash over the sides of the filter paper. The brownish liquid had tiny grains suspended in it as it was slowed down by the paper. Drop by drop, the water filtered through clear and landed in a glass jar below. What remained behind in the filter paper looked like one of my bad attempts at preparing a multi-grain bread. I poured the rest of the watery mixture into the funnel and waited patiently.

I didn't attract the same audience as before. This time only Sharry chose to come over with a cup of coffee and park herself in the stool across from me.

"What'cha doin'?" she asked conversationally.

"Testing another substance," I replied.

"Which one?" she asked.

"Well, actually, if I knew which substance it was, I wouldn't have to test it," I said, hoping I sounded sincere and not sarcastic. "What I'm doing is taking a few drops of the filtrate, the stuff that went through the filter paper, and putting it on a glass plate."

"Why?" It wasn't a stupid question.

"I need to know how many components there are to this particular evidence that I found," I explained.

"How can you tell by looking at it? It looks like water to me," Sharry said as she eyeballed the clear liquid on the plate.

"Good point. It'll take a while for the water to evaporate and then if there was anything dissolved in the water, I'll know because it might fall out of solution, so to speak," I said.

"Oh, I get it," she said.

"While you're here, Sharry, I have a question for you. Where does everyone sleep?" I asked.

"East wing, second floor. Why? Something wrong with your room?"

"No, nothing like that," I said quickly. "I'm just thinking about who could have heard Olive's screams."

"I'm not a good person to ask," Sharry said. "I could sleep through anything."

Fair enough. My room was in the west wing. I was sleeping close enough to hear the screams, I thought. I could still hear Patty's screams ringing in my head. I couldn't believe it had been less than twelve hours since this whole thing had begun. What a vacation!

I looked at the remains of the gritty substance, trapped by the filter paper. It took a while for both to dry. I turned on the stove again and heated up the glass plate a bit to hurry up the process. The coffee filter paper dried back into a warped shape. Sharry hadn't budged. *This has to be better than TV,* I thought.

"Why are you smiling?" Sharry asked.

"Am I?" I was. This was too cool. I looked over to one of the refrigerators and grabbed a magnet. I held it over the gritty substance and smiled even more when I saw what happened. There was more to this mixture than met the eye.

The magnet had extracted several tiny black-and-orange-stained elongated crystals.

"Now what in the world would you think this is?" I asked Sharry, totally tickled with the results.

"Looks like rusted iron to me," she said, unimpressed.

"That's right. But what's so cool about it is that I found it at the crime scene. It was somehow involved," I said enthusiastically.

"How do you figure?" she asked, trying to keep up with me.

"I'll let you know as soon as I have an

answer," I said.

"Gotcha." With that she got up and headed to the fireplace to collect her sweaters and jacket. "There's a driveway full of snow that needs plowing now," she said.

"I didn't think you even had a plow. You weren't using one earlier," I said to her back.

"We've got one all right, but good ol' Norm was parked in front of the garage. Before I could open it up to get to the plow, I had to clear a path for his truck," she said as she bundled into her jacket.

"Uh-huh." I was caught up in examining the white grains I discovered on the glass plate.

The door slammed behind her.

"So what do you think it is?" a voice said from behind me. It was Norm.

"Let's put it this way. I'm not certain yet," I said quietly.

"But if you had to say what it was, what would be your guess?" he pressed.

"No comment at this time," I said politely, hoping he would bug off.

He did.

I wrote: *gritty substance: sand, iron filings, and salt. What's it doing in a freezer?*

I looked over at Patty. She seemed lost in her work, tasting one sauce and then adding something, writing notes and then scratching them out. I never knew cooking was so intense.

She chopped up a tomato and then added it to the saucepan. She stirred up the mixture. I looked in the pan. I saw green onions simmering in olive oil. The tomatoes mixed in colorfully. Patty then added a spoonful of vinegar and a third cup of sugar. The oil hissed as she stirred up a storm. She wrote more notes.

I stationed Miro at the counter. "Don't let anyone near this area," I ordered her softly. She sat alert and ready. I ran up to use the plumbing in my room. On a whim, I looked down the hall. There was no one in sight. I shivered suddenly. Good grief, it was cold.

What if I took a quick peek in the room that had the light on last night? Sure, why not?

The door wasn't locked. Inside, it looked just like my room, but I liked the patterns on my drapes better. I nosed around. The room was unoccupied. The windows were shut tight. There was nothing special about it— nothing special, until I stepped in a puddle of water on the carpet.

My first instinct was to look up at the ceiling to see if the roof was leaking. No, things looked pretty dry there. I stooped over, sniffing the carpet for any odor. There didn't seem to be one. I wondered where the liquid had come from. It seemed strange that an unoccupied room would have water on the floor. I sniffed again.

"It seems like you're getting to be more and more like your dog, Detective Cardoni," Caesar said in his deep voice. I almost jumped out of my skin.

"Why did you sneak up on me like that?" I yelled.

"I didn't know you were in here. I saw the door open, saw you, and said the first thing that occurred to me."

"I don't recommend you do that again," I said with as much dignity as I could muster.

"Me neither," he grunted as he left the room.

I couldn't tell if he meant the sneaking up on me or if he was referring to my canine sniffing behavior. His voice drifted from down the hall. "There's a phone call for you."

I shut the door and hustled down to the kitchen. The hallway was as quiet as a library. The lobby was, too. Miro barked when she saw me enter the kitchen. Everything looked okay. She hadn't budged. The music was blaring. The noise of chopping and clattering of pots and pans was almost deafening.

Caesar had beaten me to the kitchen. His muscular arms were busy stirring up a storm at one of the large gas stoves. He didn't even look at me, but rather turned his back to the phone at Olive's desk as I plopped in the chair. It didn't matter what they heard at this point. I had been seen on my knees sniffing like a dog. Oh well.

It was Dr. Lawson again.

"It looks like we're going to be delayed. The snowplow almost ran into a deer in the road. The driver's pretty shook up and swore that he would need at least an hour lunch to recover."

I'll bet I knew the deer.

12

Patty

By NOW IT WAS 1:00 P.M. The pace had picked up in the kitchen. The aroma of crushed garlic filled the room. It mingled pleasantly with rosemary and nutmeg and all the other spices swirling around in the air. The roar from my empty stomach was so loud I jumped.

The chefs sat together at the table, eating lunch. They hardly paid me any notice. This time, they didn't offer me any food. I was certainly the enemy here. *Hey, Cardoni, we're finishing up a plate of such-and-such. Come join us.* In my dreams. Who would invite a detective who suspects you of murder?

A motor sputtered and died outside in the driveway. It was Sharry, done plowing.

I rummaged around with the equipment absentmindedly. I found an unopened box of crackers in my kit bag and devoured them. Miro plopped down on the floor by my feet.

It was time to resume my investigation. Coincidentally, the room was clearing. The long benches on either side of the table scraped against the floor as everyone rose. I approached Patty and asked if she wouldn't mind if I interviewed her.

"What for?" she asked. "I don't know anything about Olive's death."

"Maybe you do, maybe you don't. You and Norm did find the body. You might have vital information that can help me crack this case."

Her eyes grew wide and then narrowed to slits. She slunk off to a window seat and drew her knees up to her chest. I sat on a stool facing her, with a view of the driveway. She hugged her knees, the perfect picture of hostility. I wondered what she had to hide.

"How long have you been working here?" I asked.

"Three years," she replied tersely.

"Where were you when Olive Souffle was murdered?" I asked.

"If I told you *when* she was murdered, I'd be able to tell you a lot more than that."

Round one to Patty.

"Good point," I said. "I'm just trying to figure out who was where at what time."

"I went to bed at ten or so last night," Patty said, her tone a bit more cooperative. "I woke up at five. I noticed the power was out so I used the stoves to make the coffee for the staff."

"What time did Norm show up?" I asked.

"I guess it was just a little bit before six," Patty said.

"What door did he use?" I asked, hoping to verify Norm's statement.

"The service door," Patty said matter-of-factly.

"Did he just let himself in?" I asked casually.

"No," she replied, sounding annoyed, "he knocked." *Knocked*, I wrote.

"So you answered the door and then what?" I asked.

Patty stood up, paced to her counter and picked up a knife to slice carrots. "We went to the freezer. He had a dolly loaded up and we had to put the food away," she said.

"Who found Olive Souffle's body first?" I asked.

Patty methodically sliced the carrots. I noticed the slightest tremor in her hands as she worked. Was I making her nervous? If so, was it because I'm a homicide detective or because I was interviewing her for this particular homicide?

"I guess we both found her body at the same time," Patty said above the sounds of chopping.

"So that's when you screamed?" I asked.

"Yes," she replied abruptly.

"That was quite a scream," I said, as if I were paying her a great compliment. "I could hear it all the way up in my room."

"I was horrified," she said. "There she was, just lying there."

"It was pretty awful," I agreed. "So you found her body around what time?"

A pause in the slicing. "I'd say at six."

"Do you know of anyone who would want to see Olive Souffle dead?" I persisted.

"She wasn't perfect, you know. She ran this kitchen like a dictator," she began.

"Are you saying that she had enemies?" I offered her this line to follow.

"Yes," she said immediately.

"Would you know who they might be?" I asked.

That hesitation again, as if she were coming up with an answer. "She and Caesar were never very close."

"Has he behaved in a way that would make you think he would be an enemy or a threat to Olive's life?"

"Well, just look at him. He's the perfect killer! Those muscular arms, those dark eyes, the way he sneaks around everywhere."

"Hmm. Did you actually observe any arguments that they might have had?"

"Olive Souffle and Caesar had a major disagreement over the way he seasoned his entrees," she said dramatically.

"So he killed her over spicy food?" I said sarcastically.

"You make it sound as though you don't believe me," she accused.

"Whether or not I believe you, I need more information to create a profile." The last thing I needed was to make a hostile witness of her. I tried a different approach.

"Look at all those trophies over there," I motioned above the mantle. "I found your name on, let's see, three of them. There are ..." I counted out loud, "sixteen. Olive Souffle must have been a great chef."

"It depends on who you talk to. Part of being a great chef is being part of a team. She was the lone-wolf type. Very independent," Patty said as if the word were an insult.

"And you don't like the independent type?" This was interesting. There was some jealousy here. Was it motive for murder? "This is the second time you've mentioned that she wasn't a team player." I wanted to add fuel to this fire.

"The hardest thing about working with her was dealing with the way she'd steal your ideas and submit them as her own either in contests or for books."

"Can you give me an example?"

"Olive Souffle stole *my* ideas on more than one occasion. I'd be lying to say that it didn't bother me," she said.

"I'm curious. How many of those trophies should be yours?" I asked.

"I should have seven more!" she exclaimed.

"Did you kill Olive Souffle?" I asked, cutting straight to the point. The question dangled in the air like the knife. Time seemed to stand still as I watched Patty's knife slowly arc its way in space, hurtling to the floor. It set up a deafening clatter as it landed.

"No, I did not," she said emphatically, picking up the knife.

"Are you all right?" I asked.

"Fine!" she fairly hissed.

"When was the last time you saw Olive alive?" I asked.

"Last night."

"Do you remember what time?" I quizzed.

"A little after eight o'clock . . . ." Her voice fell.

"What was she doing?" I continued.

"Working at her desk like she always does," Patty said more quietly.

"Where was everyone else?" I needed to know if someone could confirm this.

"In the office upstairs. It's above the lobby area," Patty said. She looked out the window and stared into space.

"How long were you with her?" I was

persistent.

"About fifteen to twenty minutes?" Why was she asking it as a question?

"Can anyone verify that?" I asked.

"Yes . . . if you can communicate with the dead."

Very funny.

"What did you discuss?" I asked as I scribbled a few lines in my notebook.

"How sick and tired I was of her constantly hogging the spotlight, having to be the center of attention. Stealing our ideas."

"Were you angry?" I asked.

"You mean was I angry enough to kill her, don't you?" she said defensively.

"You tell me."

"She stole my *Perfect Pain Perdu*!" Patty exclaimed.

At my blank look she explained, "*Pain* is the French word for bread and *perdu* is the French word for lost. It's a special dish that incorporates bread, tomatoes, lettuce, and vegetables. There's so much other stuff involved that the bread seems to disappear."

Oh, right, so Olive was killed over a sandwich?

"Olive submitted it to the Seven Minute Chef Club and won Highest Honors. She won *that* trophy for *my* idea." There was enough acid in her tone to jump start a car, or melt a trophy.

"So you had an argument," I urged her on.

"We yelled . . . I yelled at her. Told her that enough was enough. She didn't deserve the trophy and the Seven Minute Chef Club watch either."

"What did Olive say?" I asked.

"She denied that it was my idea. She said that Walter had a new idea and wanted her to try it out to perfect it, give it that Olive Souffle flair."

Hmm . . . Walter?

"What happened then?" I asked.

"She raised her hand to strike me and I grabbed the watch. We struggled," she said.

"Where is the watch now?" I wondered.

"I don't know."

There was silence in the kitchen. A timer went off, clanging loudly. We both jumped. Patty walked over to the stove to turn it off.

"Did you actually take it?" I asked directly.

She turned and looked me square in the eye. "No! I didn't kill her, either!"

"Do you know who might have?"

"Isn't that *your* job, detective?" She returned to stirfrying. She was done with me.

"Do you mind if I fingerprint you?" It was worth a shot.

"Go right ahead. After I'm done with this. Perhaps you would like to be my guinea pig for this new sauce I'm perfecting?"

Perhaps not. Who knew what extra ingredient might be in it?

"Thank you, but I've got to get to the bottom of this." I walked away. On impulse I turned and asked, "May I have your pen for just a moment?"

"Certainly."

I had another experiment to do. I put a dab of ink on a strip of coffee filter paper. I wrote her name on the strip. I would ask the others for theirs as well.

"What is that for?" Patty asked, her eyes narrowed to suspicious slits again.

"I'm just going to fingerprint you and then your pen."

It would be a long process, but I would know if a pen at this lodge had been used to write the threatening note and the circle around the word *pois* on the order list.

Patty washed her hands and said, "I'm ready for fingerprinting."

Her fingers were warm and rosy.

13

Who Is the Real Caesar Martinez?

CAESAR HADN'T looked over once the whole time I had been talking to Patty. He was out of earshot and hadn't leaned our way or even wandered over as an excuse to hear our conversation. Maybe he had something to hide, maybe not. I would soon find out. I watched him carefully as I walked over. He was upset about something.

"Listen," he said, "I'm missing a shish kabob prong." He opened up a drawer and pointed. "They're kept together. Right *there*. One's missing."

"I appreciate your honesty." Honesty would be a welcome change from Patty's hostility.

He shut the drawer and opened another, as if hoping to find the missing shish kabob skewer. "I think someone's trying to set me up, make it look like I committed murder."

"Did you?" It was an interesting ploy: come clean with a confession then make it look like someone else is conveniently setting you up. Original. I liked it.

"No. I could never raise my hand to hurt another human being." My eyes strayed from his large hands to his bulging biceps. I looked inside the drawer. It was filled with different sized mallets.

"What are all those for?" I asked.

"Mallets? I pound on steaks to tenderize the meat." I shuddered for two reasons: I'm a vegetarian and, right, he could never raise his hand to . . .

"You know, Patty says that Olive had a nasty habit of stealing other people's ideas," I ventured.

"That's a lie!" he almost shouted.

Okay. My mutating conspiracy theory got tossed. Maybe.

"She was a great chef and a superb human being. She was generous and kind," he volunteered.

"So, you were friends?" I asked.

"Yes!" he answered emphatically. He was in another drawer, rummaging around.

"You agreed on everything from politics to, say, spices?"

"No, Olive Souffle didn't like my particular use of spices," he admitted.

"Too much? Too little?" I persisted.

"Too little," he said.

Patty was 0-for-2 here, unless, of course, Caesar had a better batting average as a professional liar.

"That's probably not enough to kill someone over, is it?"

"I hope not." He slowed his searching movements in the drawer. "I think that . . ." In his hand was a ladies' gold watch with a diamond at the seven. It was Olive Souffle's watch from the Seven Minute Chef Club.

He held it up like a treacherous voodoo doll that threatened to burn his hand.

"That was planted!" he almost wailed as he dropped it on the counter. His pupils dilated from a rush of adrenaline.

Or maybe you do an excellent job of looking like you're being framed, I thought as I watched him.

"You're probably thinking that I'm very good at looking like I'm being framed," he said.

"Don't you think it's odd that we would be discussing the murder and you claim that you're being set up—"

"I am!" he nearly shouted.

"—and don't you find it odd that as you're discussing it, the watch shows up?"

"I do!"

"You're either very good at deception or someone really is setting you up,"

I concluded.

"I'd put my money on door number two," a familiar voice said from the doorway. We both turned. It was Sam. He looked at us pointedly and then turned on his heel. How long had he been listening?

I heard a shuffling sound behind me and shifted my attention back to Caesar.

I faced a sleek shiny blade, about twelve inches long. He held it dangerously close to my throat.

"Do you think I could do something murderous with this?" he asked, leaning closer. His breath smelled lightly of garlic and. . . I couldn't place it. . . cloves perhaps?

"I don't know. Anyone is capable of anything given the right or the wrong circumstances," I said quietly, not moving. No need to agitate him. It would take one false move to slice and dice my jugular.

He said calmly, "Do you see this? I deal with these all day! There's no way I could ever kill someone with it!"

"Caesar!" Sharry shouted from across the room, "put it down!" She walked up from the lobby entrance with a pleading look on her face.

"I'm a peaceful guy. I don't settle my differences with murder," he spat. The knife clattered to the counter, rocking wildly.

"And you think you've made a point?"

I asked with icy sarcasm. "I carry a gun every day. I'm not going to take it out and wave it around in the hopes of intimidating you or convincing you of my opinion."

He stared at me, palms on the counter, shoulders hunched up to his ears.

"We all make choices, Caesar. Even peaceable people make foolish decisions." There was silence. "I want your pen," I said. "And then I'll take your fingerprints."

He handed over his pen with a look of more than mere curiosity. As he looked on, I spotted a strip of coffee filter paper with the ink. I labeled the paper at the top with his name.

"What can you tell me about Olive Souffle's interactions with the other cooks?" I asked.

"There's not that much to tell, really. She liked to work alone. If she was working on something with you, you hoped you did it the way she wanted it done, or she made you feel about two inches tall," he said.

"Would she yell at people?"

"No, it was more of an attitude thing. She'd look at you, real quiet-like, when your bread or your pastries didn't turn out just right," he said. "To my mind, that was worse than yelling."

"Who do you think would stand to gain the most from her death?" I asked.

"Honestly, I couldn't think of someone who *wouldn't* benefit from her death, except maybe the resort guests. In spite of the fact that she was tough to get along with, she was an incredible cook and the guests love—loved her," he said softly.

"Did Olive ever mention making any big purchases to you?" I asked, trying to make my voice sound casual. "Like land or a house or anything?"

"I don't know anything about that. You could probably ask Bert Paltry about land in the area. He's been here as long as the renovated lodge has been hosting the guests. He knows pretty much everyone in the area as well as their family histories," Caesar stated.

"I'll make a point to talk to him," I said as I looked at the stained coffee filter paper in front of me. I would test it now.

"What are you doing?" he asked as he watched me pour a small amount of distilled water into a clean measuring cup.

"You'll see," I said mysteriously. I love the clues that I retrieve from science. I reached for the scissors on the counter and trimmed off two triangular corners from the coffee filter strips. The sample ink dots balanced in the middle of each triangle. The strips resembled the tops of picket fences. I placed the strip from Patty's pen into the water, triangle end first. Then I placed Caesar's into the water. I was careful to ensure that the water would not directly touch the ink dots but rather seep up into the filter paper.

"So, what are you doing?" Caesar asked again.

"Yes, by all means, tell us what you are doing, detective." It was Walter, standing at the doorway. I hated the way he and Sam had snuck up to the doorway and not made a sound. Those doors sure did a good job of keeping the kitchen noise in the kitchen. I thought about it for a second. That would make sense. A guest enjoying a four-star meal in the dining room off the lobby wouldn't want to be disturbed by kitchen noise.

What am I missing here? I thought. Something was nagging my brain.

Patty walked over. Where had she been when Caesar had held the knife to my throat? Anyway, I had lost my train of thought.

"What are you doing?" she asked softly.

"I'm testing to see if a brand of pen on these premises was used to write a threatening note to Olive Souffle," I answered.

"You're joking," Walter said. He sounded miffed.

"Dead serious." I fixed him with an even stare across the counter.

"How does it work?" Caesar asked.

"The coffee filter paper acts as a wick, because it draws up the water. As the water travels up the paper, it carries parts of the ink that are more easily dissolved in the water. The farther a part of the ink travels, the more soluble in water it is, and the smaller it is on a molecular level."

"Why are you testing *these* pens?" Walter asked pointedly.

"Because I haven't had the opportunity to test everyone's yet," I replied.

"Here's mine," he offered.

"Thank you," I said as I looked at my watch. Five minutes had passed since I had begun the test. I would place each ink sample in the distilled water for the same amount of time.

"What is this experiment called?" Patty asked.

"Paper chromatography. *Chromo* for color and *graphy* for a picture of something. What I'm doing is essentially taking a picture of what's inside each pen, a fingerprint, as I mentioned earlier."

Patty's ink sample ran the brightest of blues that faded like a comet's tail toward the end of the test strip. Caesar's pen sample hadn't budged.

I thought about the writing style of the note. It had been written with a slant to the right. I wasn't going to put any money on it, but my hunch was that a right-handed writer had sent this to Olive Souffle. We had documents experts at P.D.'s Crime Lab who could venture a more expert guess. I was just out to see if there was a match among the staff. I wouldn't test Walter's until I was done with the first two.

After eight minutes had elapsed, the water had traveled almost to the end of the strips, carrying with it the pigments of the original ink dot. I took them out and left them to dry.

Walter stood by, waiting impatiently. Caesar watched as I tested the strip with Walter's name on it. The water migrated up the strip, piggybacking ink pigments. It bled into three different colors, a blue, red, and a purple.

"What does that mean?" Patty asked, frowning when she saw the strip drying on the counter.

"It means that Walter uses permeable ink. It dissolves in water. It also means that if you get it on your skin it's easy to wash off with soap and water. Caesar's pen is the exact opposite."

"Well done, Detective Cardoni," Walter said mockingly. With that he sauntered out of the kitchen.

"What do my results mean?" Patty asked.

"The pen you are currently using is

composed of blue pigments, a uniform mixture, because I can only make out the one color. It also means that it is easily soluble in water."

Patty seemed satisfied with this explanation and walked away.

"Anything else, detective?" Caesar asked subdued.

"Not for now. If I need more information from you, I'm sure neither one of us will feel a need to meet with weapons drawn."

He harumphed at that one.

"Okay if I get a fingerprint card on you?" I asked.

"I guess so," he said.

I was done in a few minutes. As he wiped his hands of the greasy ink I had used to fingerprint him, he looked at me carefully.

"So what if the pens here bleed a certain way? People aren't attached to their pens. Anyone could have taken one of them and used it to write the note and then put it back."

"I know," I said, fully aware of the logic. "But it will tell me if a type of pen found here was used."

Caesar was a puzzle to me, I thought as I jotted some notes in my notebook. He had seemed so adamant about not killing Olive Souffle. He seemed intelligent. He was passionate about his innocence and yet that same passion had shown itself in a foolish gesture.

I looked outside at the sun fading quickly. A bluish glow seemed to stain the snow where shadows lay. I was running out of time. So, Cardoni, how many chefs does it take to kill Olive Souffle?

14

A Crystal-Clear
Picture

IT WAS 3:30 P.M. "The medical examiner
will be here shortly," I said to the assembled.
I hoped I was even remotely close to the
truth. "In the meantime I will need a pen
sample from each of you as well as a hair."

They all looked at each other. I think it was
the first time I could sense an honest
response out of any of them. How refreshing.
They were such a tough group. If I had each
of them in the interrogation room, things
would be different.

"You can't take a hair from us!" Walter
protested.

"Under these circumstances, yes, I can.
I don't even need a search warrant. I have
probable cause and you are all under
suspicion of murder." There. I had said it.
The cards were on the table.

"What if I don't want to give a hair

sample?" Walter asked defiantly.

"It raises suspicion. Do you have something to hide?" I asked. He looked uncomfortable. "I can always get a court order and you will *have* to give me a sample," I said.

"Just help her out with this, man," Sam said, sounding disgusted with Walter's behavior. "Here. Here's one of my hairs. I don't have anything to hide, either. Here's my pen. I've had it since I started working here. I'm more of a computer note-taker, so it doesn't get much use."

Slowly, the others followed suit. I tagged everything with masking tape labels of their names. The hair samples wound up in tiny plastic bags. I would use a magnifying lens to figure out if the hair I found on Olive's body belonged to anyone in this room. It wouldn't necessarily identify the killer, but it would certainly place the individual in the freezer before I got there.

"If that's it, Cardoni," Caesar said as he walked toward the lobby door.

"We've got a meeting to get started soon," Patty said as she followed.

Soon, I was alone again with Miro. The sun was gone and there was little difference between snow and shadows. It would be dark soon. Suddenly I felt an urgency to complete the investigation. I shifted into high mental gear as I worked the coffee filter trials. The paper chromatography would be done in about ten minutes.

I noticed Sharry at the end of the long table, sipping another cup of coffee.

"Do you like your job, Sharry?" I asked impulsively.

"What's not to like?" she asked sounding surprised. "I'm my own boss. I come and go as I please. I do my work outside, in the snow, sun, rain. It's great. I get to work with tools. They're more grown-up toys for me than anything."

I nodded, listening, trying to find some useful information from her words. I walked over to the service door entrance.

"Is anyone else as outdoorsy as you are?" I asked.

She shook her head no.

"Is this where everyone leaves their stuff?"

She nodded yes.

"Which jacket is Olive Souffle's?" I asked on impulse.

"That green one to your right," she indicated.

I looked on the inside, on the lining. There were a few of Miro's hairs scattered about.

Bang. There it was. Olive had gone outside after I had seen her last night. Some of Miro's hairs had gotten on her sweater, and those hairs had been transferred to the lining of her jacket when she had put it on. I said nothing to Sharry.

"So, everyone's stuff is here, and you said everyone sleeps in the east wing, right?" I continued.

"East wing, upstairs," Sharry confirmed.

I had been in the west wing. Still no answer to the question of who was in the room down the hall from me.

"Anything else I can help you with, detective?" Sharry asked as she began to get up.

"No, thanks." I watched her zip up her jacket and put on her gloves. "What are you going to do now?" I asked her.

"There are still a few patches I've got to take care of," she said.

I took out the paper chromatography strips. My blood chilled. Walter's tricolor strip matched the sample I had taken from the threatening note.

"Mind if I join you for some fresh air?" I asked, not wanting to be alone suddenly.

"Suit yourself," she said matter-of-factly.

"Miro. Wanna go for a walk?" I asked.

At the word *walk* she sat up quickly and whine-barked. She had been cooped up in a noisy kitchen with a bunch of psycho chefs. I'm sure it would get to any dog.

I watched my breath hit the air, a foggy cloud against the darkening sky. I stood on the ramp, watching Sharry shovel a pile of snow out of the way. Miro barked wildly as she ran from one side of the driveway to the other.

I looked around. The icicles from the eaves sparkled a dull white. They were the result of snow melting from the roof, then freezing in the cold night air.

"Look out!" Sharry cried out.

I heard a whooshing noise go by my ear, and then I saw the icicle land, point first, in a pile of snow.

"Are you all right?" she said as she rushed over to me.

"I'm fine," I said.

"Gotta watch these darn things," she muttered vehemently.

I was suddenly inspired. "You know, you are absolutely right, Sharry." I quickly went inside while she started to knock them down with her shovel.

I went to the freezer and unlocked it. I left the door ajar as I covered every inch of the freezer with the beam of my flashlight. I stared at the frozen puddle near the body, determined to understand how everything had happened.

When I felt I had a crystal-clear picture of how the murder weapon had been used, I went to the door. It was shut tight.

I was locked in.

15

Just Desserts

I YELLED AND SCREAMED as loudly as I could. I wondered if they were working or standing in the kitchen. Looking at each other and pretending not to hear me. I could see the headlines. I wondered where Miro was.

Suddenly, I was getting very sleepy. "You can't get sleepy on me now, Cardoni," I thought I heard a voice say.

"But I'm so tired," I protested crankily.

"What happens to a body in cold weather, Cardoni?" the voice continued. It sounded like Juan Antonio's. I must be delirious.

"Rigor mortis, freezing, joints seizing up. The cold lowers the body temperature. It gets colder, so cold that normal chemical reactions cease to function. Blood freezes. . . ." Then darkness.

Everything seemed to happen in slow motion. Their voices were coming from a distance.

We have decided that you killed Olive Souffle . . . We were all doing just fine before you showed up, Cardoni . . . No one here has a bad bone in their body.

They descended on me like wolves on a kill.

I shook, hard and quick. I was dreaming. I was developing a pretty severe case of hypothermia. If someone didn't let me out soon, I would freeze to death. Blackness came again.

". . . hey."

I was hearing voices.

"Hey . . . wake up."

Someone was shaking me by the shoulders.

"Cardoni, wake up!" A voice called me from so far away, it seemed to come from another planet. I heard loud barking. Things scraped and shuffled.

I couldn't move my legs or arms. My mouth felt frozen in place. I was still trapped in the nightmare.

"Cardoni, don't you dare take off! Wake up!"

I recognized the voice. It was filled with panic.

"Get me some blankets here!"

What was going on? Another dream? It was too cruel. I wanted to sleep, I was so tired. I was so exhausted I didn't have the energy to wake up. I was too cold.

I grunted, protesting.

"She's alive!" the voice crowed.

I heard rapid footsteps scurrying about.

Arms lifted me gently, and I was carried out of the dark cave that had almost killed me.

Bright lights behind my eyelids. I squinted and then gave up. It was too much all at once.

A whistle-whine from my left told me Miro was there.

"Miro," I squawked.

She plowed into me and licked my face. Her tongue felt warm and rough. I tried to hug her, weakly.

I opened my eyes. I was surrounded by the cooks. Oh no, not again.

Then I saw Dr. Lawson.

"Don!" I said hoarsely. "You're really here!"

"You just get warmed up now, Cardoni," he said reassuringly as he patted my arm. I was up on a counter. The lights in the kitchen were all blazing. A fire was roaring in the fireplace and Miro was close by. Everything was okay.

"I am so sorry," Sharry began. "I shut and locked that door. I figured someone had left it open." Her face was filled with concern and anxiety.

"Didn't you think to look inside?" Dr.

Lawson said indignantly.

"There's a dead body in there! I wasn't interested in looking inside," Sharry said.

"There could have been *two* dead bodies if we hadn't gotten here when we did," Dr. Lawson said as Bert Paltry appeared and nodded his head vigorously.

"You're lucky the Doc here came to my store," Bert said as he leaned over the counter. His breath was pepperminty. "He showed up about twenty minutes ago, huh. I offered to bring him over here."

He looked at me pointedly. "Just wondered if we could get my store's name in the article, if there is one, you know. It would help business some."

What a cheap publicity hound. What a low-level form of life. What a poor excuse for human DNA. What a nice guy for helping save my life.

"Dr. Lawson, what do you think about the body?" I asked as I began to focus again.

"I haven't really had a chance to look at it, Cardoni. I was set on helping you first," he said. "Are you going to be okay here?" he asked, concerned, tucking the blanket around my shoulders.

Sharry said, "Don't worry, I'll watch her."

"Better than last time, right?" he said as he walked toward the freezer.

She blushed a deep red and said to me

fiercely, "I'll never be able to apologize enough. All I can say is that I am sorry."

"Where was everybody?" I asked, dusting off my conspiracy theory.

"We were in a meeting in the office," Patty said as she walked past. She turned a dial on the stove and an alarm went off briefly. I looked at the time. It was 7:00 P.M. Was I really out for that long? Patty took out a tray of brownies. My stomach growled.

"Oh, this is for you, Cardoni," Dr. Lawson said. It was pizza, vegetarian, from Tomaso's Pizza Grotto in town. It was cold, but I was hungry. Miro trotted over.

Sam asked, "What do we have for Miro?"

"Cold cuts," Caesar answered.

"Biscuits," Patty chimed in.

"Crackers?" Sharry said, sounding uncertain.

The list went on.

"Split pea soup," Walter said.

Wait a minute. I frantically searched my pockets for the envelope that held Olive Souffle's grocery list. I found it and looked at all the items. I looked at the word *pois* that had been circled. *Pois* means "pea" in French. Pea . . . as in pea soup—or Walter Peace?

16

Bon Appetit!

IT WAS 10:30 P.M. Norm was trying his hand at a crossword puzzle. He seemed frustrated, impatient.

"What's another word for foreshadowing?" he asked the others, who hardly paid him any notice.

The others had returned to their places around the table and were discussing the opening of the inn and their recipes. Dr. Lawson was busy examining the body.

I was feeling better and was testing the fingerprints from the back of the gold watch that Patty had ripped from Olive's wrist. I looked at the results. They matched Patty's and Caesar's. This made sense. Both of them had handled the watch.

I still had the threatening note. Who would have written Olive Souffle such a thing? I looked over to Norm working the puzzle and got another flash of inspiration. Why not get a handwriting sample from everyone?

I got up and ripped out sheets of paper from my notebook. "Could you all write something down for me?" I asked as I handed each person a sheet. Everyone wrote their names in the upper-right-hand corner and waited for my next instruction. I got them all to write the exact words that were written on the death threat note. I collected their writing samples.

Everything fell into place.

At that moment Dr. Lawson walked out of the freezer.

"I've got a story to tell, Don," I told him.

"I'm listening," he said as he snapped his case shut and sat down at the table. The cooks gathered around.

"Olive Souffle was killed sometime between 12:40 Thursday morning when I last saw her and 6 in the morning, when Norm and Patty found the body. The evidence I found in the freezer and in the kitchen gave me a great deal of information about the circumstances surrounding her death.

"I noticed a large bump on Olive's left temple when I examined the body. Does the bump on Olive Souffle's head seem to have been made by a heavy weight, such as a bag of sugar, Dr. Lawson?"

"That theory *would* be supported by the mark on her head," he said.

"Indeed. She had been knocked over the

head by a heavy bag of sugar. I know this because I tested the white, crystalline solid that I found near her hair."

I looked around the room. "The bag might have even broken and scattered sugar all over the place. It didn't matter. This is a working kitchen. No one would think a few sugar grains on the floor was anything unusual.

"I also found a grocery list crumpled up in Olive's pocket. Circled on the list was the word *pois*. *Pois* is the French word for peas. I wondered if that meant *Peas* as in *Walter Peace*?"

I looked at Bert. "Bert was kind enough to tell me that Olive was about to buy this lodge and the abandoned gold mine from Paris Peace, Walter's father."

All eyes were on Bert and then Walter.

"I had a serious motive for Walter," I said. "He wanted to develop the area into a tourist trap, with water slides, tours of the cave and the mine, the works. The only problem for Walter was that his father had other plans for the area, plans that seemed more in keeping with what Olive wanted to do with the land. Olive saw a nature preserve, a retreat of sorts shaping up around the lodge and the gold mine."

"I did not kill Olive Souffle," Walter said emphatically.

"But someone wanted us to believe that you killed her. Someone planted a black hair at the scene that perfectly matches your hair and no one else's. I examined a sample from each of you. Walter, yours does match the one found on Olive's shirt."

"But I didn't kill Olive Souffle!" he exclaimed.

"I didn't say that you did," I said calmly. "Motive and planted evidence don't mean murder."

I continued. "The killer didn't count on Walter being allergic to dogs. There's no way that the hair on Olive's sweater could be his. He'd have broken out into hives or watery eyes. He couldn't have been at the scene earlier because Miro's hair was all over Olive Souffle's sweater. I don't know where the killer got the hair, but it doesn't put Walter at the scene."

They all seemed to be trying to absorb this.

"I also found Olive Souffle's pen in her pants pocket. I tested it using paper chromatography. It had been used to circle the word *pois* on the grocery list. It's a funny thing, though. I found her pen in her right pants pocket."

"So?" Sam asked.

I turned to him. "Where did you put your pen now that you're done with the writing sample I asked for?"

"In my right pocket," he answered.

"Which hand do you write with?"

"I'm right-handed."

"Olive Souffle was left-handed," I stated.

There was silence.

"So you're saying someone faked her circling the word *pois*?"

"It would appear that way."

They listened intently as I continued. "Patty says that she went to see Olive and argued with her."

At this, Patty hung her head.

"When Olive and I spoke the night I arrived, Olive wasn't wearing a watch. In the morning when I examined her body, there was a circular bruise on her right wrist. Patty says that they had an argument and that she took Olive's watch."

"But I didn't kill her!" Patty exclaimed.

I ignored her and went on. "The watch turned up in one of Caesar's equipment drawers."

"I didn't kill Olive," Caesar protested.

"The watch had Caesar's and Patty's fingerprints on it. There are three options here. Either Patty planted the watch, Caesar put the watch there himself, or someone else put the watch there while wearing gloves. We're going to eliminate the possibilities one by one.

"How many of you were awakened by

Patty's screams?"

Everyone nodded yes. There were murmurs of *me, I was.*

"Could you all come with me?" I asked.

Curious, they followed. Miro trotted by my side. I told her to stay by the lobby door and we all filed up to the second floor of the east wing.

Miro's whistle-whine faded as we went up the stairs.

"Miro, *spritz*!" I ordered. Talk! It was a close approximation of the German word.

She howled the way only an ancient relative of a wolf could. It made the hair on my neck stand up as it always did.

"So what's your point?" Sam asked, somewhat disturbed by the demonstration.

"Just wait," I said as I ran downstairs, past Dr. Lawson's smiling face.

"Miro, inside," I ordered as she moved into the kitchen. We walked to the freezer door and stood outside it. "Miro, *spritz*!"

She did and the howl filled the kitchen.

"Stay!" She grunted and lay down obediently.

I returned to the group sitting on the stairs of the second flight of the east wing.

"Did you hear that?" I asked as I rejoined them.

"Hear what?" Sharry asked.

"Did you hear anything the whole time I

was gone?" I asked, excited as I always get when the picture comes into focus.

"Not a darn thing huh," Bert muttered. "Are you losin' it?"

"Patty, could you go downstairs and scream the way you did this morning?" I asked her.

She walked down the steps slowly and disappeared around the wall.

I urged everyone to follow quietly.

We stood at the bottom of the stairs, at one end of the lobby. Our footsteps were muffled by the heavy carpeting and drapes.

Suddenly Patty screamed. They all jumped.

"Look!" I exclaimed.

She had been standing at the door of the kitchen, projecting her scream to the lobby and the east and west wings.

"Why would you scream there?" I asked. "Hadn't you found the body in the freezer?"

She started slightly. She hadn't thought we'd be standing right there. She had no answer for me.

"What was the story you were planning to tell? Let's see. Your battery-powered alarm clock went off. You came downstairs as you always do at five-thirty. When you came downstairs this morning, you helped Norm in with a delivery. You both saw the body in the freezer and then you screamed."

Everyone circled around her in the lobby, looking at her.

I turned to Patty. "But that's not the story, is it? Was it because you had fought with Olive and felt guilty? I wonder if it was because you were a part of this whole murder and were worried you would be implicated in it."

No words from Patty.

"The frozen liquid that I found on the freezer floor really made me think. It looked as though it could have been blood when I began to test it," I continued as they listened attentively.

"It looked like it to me," Walter chimed in.

"When I tested it, the physical properties were obvious: This was mostly a clear substance that boiled at around 100 degrees Celsius, had no distinct odor, and had a density of 1 gram per milliliter and a neutral pH. I told Sharry she was basically drinking it."

"You mean water?" said Caesar.

Sharry nodded her head yes.

"Exactly," I said.

"But if it was water, how come it was red?" Walter asked.

"That's the same question I kept asking myself!" I exclaimed. "I was watching Sam mix a batch of icing and later watched him ice a cake when it *hit* me. He had handed me a knife that had a trace amount of red food coloring on it, so small that I couldn't see it. I used that knife to pick up the frozen water off the freezer floor. The red food coloring on the blade contaminated the sample that I collected. The ice melted in the kitchen and so the sample looked like blood."

Sam blushed a deep crimson.

"Someone wanted to make certain that Olive Souffle would die and so they used a sharp, pointed instrument to stab her through the heart."

All eyes turned to Caesar. He was still missing the shish kabob prong. He looked as though he wanted to run away.

"Are you still missing the kabob stick?" I asked him.

"Yes," he said rather grimly.

"Well, it looks like someone took that to make it look like you had stabbed her."

"Well, I didn't!" he exclaimed.

"The killer did something calculating, something brilliant. He or she grabbed hold of an icicle from the eave of the roof and walked into the freezer and stabbed Olive Souffle," I said and watched their faces.

Sharry's eyes drew wide in awe. Walter looked decidedly green.

"Can you confirm that, Dr. Lawson?" I asked.

"Based on the evidence at the scene," he said, "I can agree with your theory. The body was already cold enough that blood wouldn't flow freely. Also, the stab wound is more consistent with an icicle rather than with a single pointed kabob stick."

The chefs nodded in interest at this new information.

"Think about it," I offered, "no fingerprints, easy disposal, probably not even enough DNA or fiber evidence to run any conclusive tests. The icicle was the perfect murder weapon."

They nodded their heads slowly.

"I saw scuff marks on the heels of Olive Souffle's shoes. Those marks could only have been made going across the floor with her being dragged backwards. She was dragged into the freezer and left to die. This led me to my next question: Where had she come from?

"I found a brown gritty substance outside the freezer. It seemed to have scuffed Olive's shoes somewhat, particularly the heels. I tested it. This gritty substance is granular, crystalline in structure. It is composed of sand particles and some sodium chloride. There was also a bit of iron and iron oxide. In other words, the gritty substance was mostly sand with some salt, or sodium chloride. It's mostly used to prevent slipping on slick, icy surfaces. The salt itself lowers the freezing point of the ice so that it doesn't slick up."

"We use that on all the steps in the winter season," Sharry interrupted.

"Thanks for confirming that," I said. I was on a roll. "The iron probably came from the sand mixture. If you go to the beach with a magnet, you can pick up a fair amount of iron filings. My guess is that Olive Souffle was dragged into the freezer from a place closer to the service door entrance—perhaps even from the outside."

They nodded their heads slightly. It seemed to make sense.

"I asked Sharry where Olive's jacket was kept. I looked inside the jacket and noticed that there were dog hairs on the inside lining. She had patted Miro several times the night we arrived. It made sense, then, that she had put on her jacket at some point in the night after I had gone to my room."

"But Olive wasn't wearing it when you found her," interrupted Caesar.

"You're right," I said. "The jacket was hanging up by the service door entrance with all the others. This made me think that Olive had taken off the jacket or someone took it off for her because she was knocked unconscious."

I looked at their faces. They were paying rapt attention to my every word.

"This led me to think that the power had not yet gone off. If it had, she would have kept her jacket on to keep warm and may have even worn it up to her room. But she hadn't. The power was still on and she had gone outside for something."

"Maybe she just needed some fresh air?" Walter suggested helpfully.

"Not quite," I replied, "I have to admit that it was all there in front of me. You see, Olive Souffle was waiting for someone. It's my guess they had called in advance to tell her that they were on their way. She was expecting someone, someone among you. Someone she trusted."

The fire sparked and spattered suddenly. No one moved.

"Olive herself told me who killed her, or actually who was *going* to kill her. I first met Olive Souffle when she came to the door and rescued me from freezing to death. Her exact words were 'Zees ees not a delivery?'"

All eyes turned toward Norm.

He frowned. "This is exactly as you said it would be, a witch hunt. All of your experiments and interviews, they were a waste of time, and now you're trying to find someone to pin the murder on," he said.

"Listen to what I have to say," I said. "I noticed footprints outside in the snow when I first arrived late Wednesday night. I figured someone had to be here. I didn't think much of the footprints at the time.

When Olive checked me in, I saw a light under the door down the hall from me.

"I didn't connect the footprints in the snow with that light until I investigated the room on Thursday. There was a puddle of water on the carpet. It was from melted snow. The killer may have been in the lodge and was hiding in the room. Maybe they turned the light on while they were getting rid of the snow that was melting into their boots. The lights went out as soon as I must have made a noise getting into my room."

"That's when I saw you checking out the puddle?" Caesar asked.

"Exactly. While Olive was heating up pea soup in the kitchen and asking me about Miro, the killer must have heard our voices and waited. When Olive showed me to my room, the killer was the one standing in the room down the hall."

They looked stunned. They looked at Norm as if he had grown two heads.

"Admit it, Norm. You called Olive Souffle and told her you would try to be there earlier because you thought the storm would delay your regular delivery by more than a day. You sounded concerned. Olive must have appreciated such consideration, especially two days before the lodge was due to open for the season. She sat up later than usual, working on a new order list. Everyone had already gone to bed. You had thought through most of it.

"After I fell asleep, you went downstairs to the kitchen. Olive was sitting there at her desk, working on the order form."

I paused while I thought through it all myself. The pieces fit better than I had guessed.

"You showed up in the kitchen and made up some story about needing her help to back the truck up to the door. She put on her jacket and went outside to wave you back as you parked. You were thinking about it. Could you murder her? You started to unload things and she went inside. You had already loaded a few items onto the dolly and you started to make your way to the freezer. At some point in the delivery, you grabbed a bag of sugar and struck her over the head. She fell unconscious. You dragged her into the freezer and left her to die. But that wasn't enough, so then you stabbed her with an icicle. Sometime in the morning Patty showed up and became a part of it."

Patty shrieked in protest.

"When I asked Patty if you had knocked at the door to make your delivery, she said yes. When I had asked *you* if you knocked, you said no, that Patty just let you in. Somewhere in this mess, the two of you became co-conspirators."

Patty was looking decidedly pale, chalky. Her mouth was slightly open, her eyes wide with terror.

"Sam, do cabbages belong in a freezer?"

"Not normally," he said from his place at the table.

"But that's what Norm was delivering into the freezer when I met him," I said. "He was trying to make it look like any other delivery.

"You hadn't planned on a few other things, Norm. We all know that Patty had to be right near the lobby entrance for that sound to carry upstairs into both wings. Why would she scream there if the body was found in the freezer?

"Another thing. You hadn't figured on the snow piling up on your truck, indicating that you had been parked somewhat hidden from view in the garage area. You had to have arrived last night before the snow really came down.

"You were there because Patty had complained to you about Olive stealing her fruited *Pain Perdu* recipe and winning an award with it. You probably felt that Patty should have won the award and gotten all the credit. You killed Olive Souffle after you heard their argument, and when Patty found out, she helped you cast suspicion on Caesar and Walter.

"Patty circled the word *pois* on the grocery

list. She knows some French. She may have also found a hair from Walter's jacket to plant on Olive Souffle's shirt. She had the watch and she may have planted it in Caesar's utensil drawer."

Norm looked at Patty, tears in his eyes.

She looked away, shaking.

"I began to suspect you, Norm, when Sam told me you had said that Olive had been stabbed. I wondered what you based this on. But it wasn't until just a while ago, that I had something to go on.

"When I looked at the handwriting samples from the threatening note, I examined the spelling of the words to figure out who wrote the note. Your difficulty with the crossword puzzle actually inspired me, Norm. I have you up for motive and a premeditated murder. You see, when I had everyone give me a handwriting sample of the threatening note, yours was the only one that matched it identically. The death threat has Olive's name spelled *s-o-u-f-l-e*. Norm, *souffle* is spelled with two fs."

EPILOGUE

It WAS OVER so suddenly. The sheriffs were sent back up and Norm Adams and Patty Bordeaux were read their rights and taken away in separate cars. There was no telling whether their stories would match. It didn't matter. They would have their day in court and Olive Souffle's story would finally end with justice.

Dr. Lawson waited with me for the rest of the homicide team to show up. They took more photographs. Then they took my statement and my report. They had never seen an icicle used as a murder weapon before. They asked a lot of questions. Of course, Bert Paltry had to hog the spotlight and stretch the truth of his involvement in solving the case.

When it was all over, the staff seemed relieved to see us all go before their real guests showed up. They didn't need any publicity of this kind. They baked and cooked furiously for the rest of the evening and early the next morning. They presented a huge care package to Miro and me. I finally got those chocolate chip cookies I had been craving when this whole thing started. I wouldn't have to cook anything after all for weeks, it looked like.

It was amazing that all this happened while I was on my way to a great vacation. I never did get to use the cookbooks, the CDs, and the oil paints I had packed. And I didn't get to go skiing. I couldn't blame the deer, though. Sometimes things happen for a reason. Yes, I missed my vacation. But I did make a new friend. Sam is coming to visit next week. He said he's going to bring a full-fledged chocolate mugging.

Actually, I made two new friends. Olive was the other one. Every time I have split pea soup, I raise my spoon in a silent salute to the classiest chef I've ever met.

Until next time . . .

Signed,

Angel Cardoni

MARGARET BENOIT has been collecting and reading books—especially mysteries—all her life. She wrote her first story in the second grade and continued to write stories, plays, and essays throughout high school.

"I love jeans, hiking, skiing, music, exercise, and going on police ridealongs," she says, "but people run for cover when I cook." Margaret, who has a masters degree in forensic science and carries a notebook for story ideas wherever she goes, admits that she's the only adult she knows who still has her high school science notes.

When she's not writing and teaching, Margaret gardens, paints, takes photographs, and tends the fish pond she dug herself. She lives in San Diego with her husband, her German shepherd, Major, and two cats.